# Witch's Medicine

## Stephanie Jones, MD
### Book 1

## A. Peche

GBSW Publishing

*Thanks to my editor Ellen Falk and my first reader GM. Neither of you were interested in following me in my pursuit in a new Urban Fantasy Series. Alas, you managed to enjoy the story and make it even better.*

# Chapter One

D r. Stephanie Jones paused to look at Lord Warrior Gormon Mialynn as she was doing her usual hustle out the door to drive to her work at the Sacramento Trauma Center.

"Are you ready for the human world?"

"Is it so different from the Elven Republic?"

"You will be the only magical person and humans are very emotional. You'll probably decide to tell your king to forget about this world and just let the prisoners run wild here."

"You forget, I am a warrior. I have many options on how to deal with difficult humans. We do have humans in our world. Not many, but I have come across them before."

"Yeah, right," she mumbled under her breath as she exited the house and approached her car in the garage.

She showed him how to put on his seatbelt and backed out of her driveway.

"Can you fly around on your home planet, or do you have a fast way to get around?"

"I can teleport anywhere I need to go. I do not fly. I do not have wings."

"You may want to close your eyes here. It might seem like we're going to crash or be crashed into at any moment."

"I will not close my eyes," Gormon said stiffly.

Stephanie smiled to herself and thought about her wild twenty-four hours. She treated some of the weirdest injuries in her career yesterday at work, had a few unexplained deaths, met Lord Warrior Gormon Mialynn from the Elven Republic, and learned that a grimoire from his world had placed itself in an old box of her medical school textbooks. The topper to the weird day was that she learned she was a witch and she agreed to help the Elven Republic collect their fifty or so escaped prisoners roaming the Earth. Yep, it was just an average day for a forty-six-year-old widowed mother and emergency medicine physician. Thankfully, her daughter was off at college and wasn't around to question her mother's sanity.

The previous evening, she had performed a variety of medical checks on herself to prove she wasn't hallucinating or otherwise experiencing an altered reality. Even as she got ready this morning for work, she wondered whether Gormon would be there in the flesh.

He'd volunteered to accompany her to work and heal patients. As a physician boarded in emergency medicine, she could think of many problems with his being there—legal, moral, ethical. He wasn't a physician, and did he even know human anatomy? He looked like a human, but with pointy ears, so she would assume they had similar anatomy.

What convinced her to letting him try healing some of her patients was the death of two patients attacked by his escaped prisoners. They used poisons or caused trauma unlike anything she had seen before in her twenty years as a fully trained physician. He wasn't prescribing medicines and wasn't doing surgery, he was simply healing people with his hands. Maybe there would be a few miracles in her emergency room today. She hoped so—every few days a patient came in with a horrible cancer, or multiple broken bones from an accident, and if her warrior friend could offer them pain relief or even accelerate their healing or diminish a tumor, that would be a win in her mind.

They worked out a spell in the grimoire whereby she could see him, because he usually used an invisibility cloak when he was moving among humans. The Elven Republic didn't want Gormon's presence to be announced to the human race. He'd crossed over onto Earth when the Elven Republic realized that an accidental avalanche-prevention detonation had caused their suspended-animation prison to reactivate and release prisoners. Gormon, with the assistance of a few other fae warriors, had teleported some of the prisoners back to the realm so they couldn't hurt Earthlings, but some had already escaped into the Lake Tahoe region. He needed help, but his home world was contending with the onslaught of prisoners and what to do with them two hundred years after sentencing. One of the prisoners whom he'd sent home was a giant who would wreak havoc back in the kingdom before he was contained.

He'd followed his senses to a fairy hiding in a mountain cabin trying to warm up. She relayed what happened in the suspended-animation prison, and he teleported her home to be reunited with her family. He continued onward until he picked up the signal of the grimoire and approached the woman. She was startled at his presence, and he was startled that she could see him. They discovered that when her hand was on the grimoire, she could see him; if she took her hand off, his invisibility spell worked.

She occasionally glanced at him while she made the twenty-minute commute to the hospital. His eyes widened on occasion at all the cars, the light rail trains, and even the airplanes overhead. He'd asked her about those, and she explained to the best of her ability. His king had warned him that Earth used technology that did some of the same things that magic did, just in a different way. Still, it was a strange world.

She pulled into the parking lot, and they exited the car. She once again went over her new spell and watched him appear and disappear before her eyes. That proved to her that hospital staff and patients wouldn't be able to see him. She sighed and walked inside just as an ambulance was arriving. She took a quick look at the patient board and saw that the department beds were about half full now. The trauma room doors were open, and staff were gathered and ready to do their best for the arriving patient.

She called out, "Dr. Perez, need any assistance? I'm here a few minutes early." She stood to

the side as the gurney rushed by and into the room.

Her colleague answered, "Yeah, take a look at the patient in room twelve."

Stephanie nodded and logged into the patient medical record computer system to see what the details were for this case. She gave the briefest of glances at Gormon to see what he was up to. He was watching the trauma room in rapt fascination. She didn't understand or trust his healing magic yet and made him promise he would approach and *heal* only patients that she approved of first.

She read a short summary of the patient, and she could see why Dr. Perez was concerned. This patient was slowly getting worse. Their vital signs were dropping, and so far, no one had found out why.

Before she completely decided what she wanted to do for the patient, she wrote a quick note to Gormon that said, *heal the patient in room 12.* She got up as if to glance at the activity in the trauma room and slapped the note into Gormon's hand. She returned to perusing the data and wondered if this patient was like her earlier patient harmed by one of the prisoners on the loose. After reviewing all the data, she walked over to the room. A nurse was on one side of the bed, and Gormon was on the other side with his hand on the patient's shoulder, his invisibility charm was keeping him hidden.

"Oh hi, Dr. Jones. Have you had a chance to review this patient's chart?"

Stephanie was happy to see it was Barbara Fox at the bedside, who was one of her favorite nurses. Friendly, competent, and caring—the best attributes of the finest nurses.

"Yes. I started my shift a little early and Dr. Perez asked me to look in on this patient. How are her vital signs?"

"In the last few minutes or so, they've been improving. I guess the medication is finally working."

"That's good to hear. Her story and symptoms sort of remind me of the hiker we had yesterday," Stephanie said, with concern in her voice.

"Me too. I suggested to Dr. Perez that we start blood pressure support sooner rather than later. Still, it's puzzling what is going on."

Stephanie watched as Gormon released the patient's shoulder and nodded. She guessed that he'd done what he could for the patient, and she certainly was doing better. She slapped another piece of paper into Gormon's hand and sent him back to the trauma room. She was curious about what he could do and if he could even get close enough to touch the patient as usually it was crowded with staff in the trauma room.

"Did you find any mysterious arrows piercing the skin?"

"Not yet, but frankly we haven't searched for them. Now that she seems to have stabilized, I'll complete my examination and talk with her. She was barely coherent when she arrived about thirty minutes ago."

Stephanie nodded and left the room confident in Nurse Fox's ability to get the full story from the patient. She was also confident that whatever Gormon had done with healing magic would counter any poison from a fae prisoner. She hated that she didn't have a good way to communicate with him. She vowed to get a phone for him so she could text him. Perhaps he could speak telepathically to her, but then she wouldn't be able to reply. She finished adding notes about her patient, then decided to check in with Dr. Perez to see if he needed any added help as they were at change of shift. The trauma room was empty, so that meant they likely had taken the patient to surgery or radiology.

She looked around for Gormon and was unable to spot him. She redid her spell to be able to see him as she questioned if spells wore off, but she still couldn't find him. She wondered if he moved with the trauma patient. While she was distracted with him, a few more patients rolled in, and she needed to refocus on the job at hand. Before she knew it, an hour passed, and she still hadn't seen Gormon. For all she knew, his king had called him back to his home planet.

Around lunch time, she had a break and grabbed a bite to eat in the physicians's lounge. Gormon entered the room and approached her. She had her answer somewhat about whether her spell wore off as it was now four hours since she'd seen him last.

She glanced around the lounge and there were another ten physicians eating their lunch, so she pulled a piece of paper out of her pocket and wrote a note.

*Give me a few minutes to finish my lunch, then follow me outside.*

He nodded and used the time to glance around the room at

the humans. It was a fascinating morning at Stephanie's hospital as she called it. He'd seen the inside of human bodies and more fluids and smells than he ever expected in his life. He'd also improved the lives of the humans he'd touched and offered his healing energy to. He'd found an area with sick children and visited all of them, providing healing. He was exhausted. He needed to eat and meditate. Stephanie stood up in his peripheral vision and he followed her outside of the dining area and down a corridor. She came to a room with a sign of a female wearing a skirt and opened the door. She held it open for him and he followed her inside the small room. There was a toilet and wash basin.

In a low voice she asked, "Where have you been? I thought my spell wore off as I couldn't see you anywhere."

"I went to the trauma room as you suggested, and that man was very sick and had likely been attacked by one of my prisoners. I stayed with him until it seemed like he would make it."

"Did you go into surgery with him?"

He nodded, and all Stephanie could think about was what kind of foreign bacteria and germs he had introduced into the operating room.

"We humans consider the operating room to be a sterile environment. We have staff wear gowns and booties, scrub their hands, and wear gloves so they don't let the bacteria on their skin contaminate a patient's wound. I'm scared to think of any foreign germs you brought with you from the Elven Republic."

Gormon had puzzled over the garments people put on and the masks. In his world, a healer healed by touch. He didn't understand the word *infection*. He would have to study it.

Stephanie was watching him and seemed to sense that he didn't understand her concern. Instead, she asked, "Was the patient alive when you left them?"

"Of course," he said, affronted.

Stephanie made a mental note to follow the patient for infection. Of course, if one of the fae prisoners had caused the wounds, how would she be able to tell the source of the infection—Gormon or the fae prisoner?

"Our methods of healing must seem quite brutal compared to yours."

"Yes. I have never seen the inside of a body before and so many people were tending to healing."

"Did you stay with that patient all morning?"

"No. I wandered around and found an area housing children, so I think I healed all of them. I am quite exhausted and need to go somewhere to meditate and regain my healing touch."

Stephanie frowned, both pleased and worried he'd healed the children in the pediatric unit. He was a warrior and carried swords. What did he know of sick kids? Then she thought back to a conversation she'd overheard but hadn't paid attention to in the physicians's lounge. The pediatricians were calling it a lucky day, as every one of their patients had improved.

"I need a way to communicate with you. As you've seen, we have lots of technology here. If I got you a phone, would you learn to use it? It won't work in your world, but it will work here unless there isn't a nearby cell tower," Stephanie asked, holding up her phone. "I can show you a text feature that will allow us to write to each other. Even if you could speak into my mind, I can't speak into yours."

Gormon looked at her phone and thought about her words. On the one hand, the phone seemed strange with words written on a screen that somehow traveled to another screen, but he couldn't argue her point.

"Yes, I will do that. I will return to my king and update him. Then I will recuperate and return later to your house. You can teach me about this phone device and cell towers. Will you have time to ask the two patients where they were attacked? We need to go hunting this evening or more humans will be injured."

"Yes, I will get details. I don't know if the patient you followed to surgery will be recovered enough to talk, but I will try."

He nodded and asked, "Anything else?"

"No, go and rest."

He disappeared in front of her eyes. She washed her hands and then left the bathroom hoping no one was waiting for it. She was pleased that the hallway was clear. It was time to return to the emergency department and see what new patients had arrived while she had lunch. She also wanted to find time to question the two patients if they were available.

She assessed the patients awaiting her attention and also checked the status of the first patient that Gormon healed. She was still stable but there were no plans to discharge her just yet. Stephanie took care of a few chest pain and pneumonia patients, and someone in a mental health crisis. Each diagnosis came with its own protocol to follow for treatment, so she didn't have to think too hard about doing all the right things for the patients. She got a break and took time to go see the woman who was their first patient that day, having likely encountered a fae prisoner.

"Hello Ms. Steckel. I'm Dr. Jones and I treated you when you first arrived at the hospital this morning. I'd like to get some more details about what happened before you arrived."

She pulled up a chair and sat facing the young woman with pen and paper in hand.

"I don't quite know what happened. I was walking around my neighborhood like I do every morning. I had my head-phones on and suddenly, I felt dizzy. I sat down on the ground and fortunately someone walking on the opposite side of the street whom I often see on my morning walks came over to see what was wrong. The next thing I knew, I woke up here."

"Were you close to your home? Had you just started your walk?"

Stephanie watched the woman think about her morning and then say, "I was a block away. Usually, I walk my dog with me, but he had a cut on his paw, so I left him at home. It was a good thing as I don't think the ambulance would have brought him with me here. I need to get out of here and go home. I usually work from home, and he'll be wondering where I am."

"Normally, we would want to observe you overnight as you came in seriously ill, but once we stabilized your vital signs, you have been good all day. Do you have a blood pressure machine at home?"

"No. I'm young and have had no blood pressure problems."

"Is there someone you could stay with or someone who could stay with you? I wouldn't discharge you if I thought you were going to have further problems; still, you should take precautions for a few more days as we don't know what caused your problems to begin with."

"I wondered if I was stung by an insect or something. I felt a slight prick in the back of my neck before I felt weird."

"Can you show me where you felt the prick? I'd like to make sure you're not having an allergic reaction there."

Stephanie examined the area that the patient pointed to at the edge of her hairline and there it was, a tiny arrow. She was grateful that Gormon's healing magic countered the poison arrow.

"Just a moment, let me grab a dermatoscope. There may be a stinger, or something stuck there, but I'd like to add light and magnification."

Jill left to grab the magnifying equipment, tweezers, and

placed a specimen cup in her coat pocket. She needed to drop the arrow into the cup without the patient seeing anything. Fortunately, with her back to Stephanie, it wouldn't be a problem.

Sure enough, when Stephanie returned and looked through the magnifying glass, she plucked the arrow out and dropped it into the cup. It was so tiny that it made no sound. She said to her patient, "Sorry, it was a hair that I saw. You do have redness in this area, so I think you were right that you might have some kind of insect bite. Are you allergic to bees?"

"Not that I know, and I don't recall hearing a bee."

"Perhaps it was an insect with some type of pollen on it that caused this reaction. I've swabbed the area, so there should be no residue left on your scalp. I will have Nurse Fox prepare your papers for discharge."

"Thank you, Dr. Jones."

She nodded and left the room. She debated whether to send the specimen cup to the lab or keep it. They already had one arrow in their possession. Maybe if she sent it with Gormon back to his world, they would learn what the poison was or who was firing the arrows. Gormon wasn't always going to be around to heal her patients, so it would be helpful if she could get a cure for the poison arrows.

The remainder of her shift was uneventful as far as the fae prisoners causing mysterious illnesses. She took a moment to log in and check on the patient who had gone to surgery. From what she read, he was still recovering from his injuries and would be unable to talk. She located the ambulance report to see where he was picked up. She now had a few points on a map of where the attacks by the fae prisoners had occurred. She signed out her shift to her colleague and was soon leaving the hospital's parking structure thinking about the fae attacks.

None of them were in suburban Sacramento. The locations

were in the counties closer to Lake Tahoe. She had the next day off and perhaps she and Gormon could drive toward the locations. When she got home from work, she was going to study her grimoire to see what useful spells she might learn. She was good at memorization, and she would need some defensive skills. She would quiz Gormon on the fighting skills of the missing prisoners. She only hoped that he would arrive at her home soon.

She paused to marvel again about what an outrageously wild day and a half it had been. She was communicating with a man from another world. She watched him heal people with only his hands. Now she was gearing up to hunt for fae prisoners that were harming her world and planning on exploiting her unknown witch talents to be an equal partner to this warrior. She was facing a dangerous and unknown future, and while she thought she should be worried; she was instead eager and excited to take on this new challenge.

# Chapter Two

Stephanie was in her kitchen cooking dinner. She'd had a brief conversation with her daughter and was making spaghetti for two in case her guest showed up. On her way home, she had purchased a cell phone to give to Gormon. After prepping a simple side salad, she began plating her dinner. No sooner had she sat down and picked up her fork, than Gormon appeared startling her.

"Hi. Would you like something to eat?"

He looked at her food and shrugged. It smelled good, but he did not recognize its appearance.

She returned to her stove and shortly placed a plate in front of him along with a glass of water. While she would have enjoyed a glass of red wine with her meal, she wanted to stay sharp for the discussion ahead.

"Any new information on the prisoners?" Stephanie asked.

"Yes and no. I have a complete list of those on the loose on Earth as well as their crimes and special skills."

"Special skills?"

"We have many kinds of fae, and they have many special talents. The worst criminal on the list is a powerful warlock."

"In books on Earth, most fantasy stories have warlocks as the good guys."

Gormon looked at her, puzzled. He was confused by her statement about stories. His king thought that humans were unaware of people from the Elven Republic. Now the good doctor said that her people were writing books about his people. What was going on?

Stephanie was watching Gormon's usually unexpressive face and noted his confusion. She thought she could guess the root of that confusion and so she tried to explain.

"In the human world, we have many books. Some books are fiction and others are non-fiction. Fiction books are stories created by a writer's imagination. They are not about facts, or, history, or say, a biography of a famous person. We have been imagining fairies in the human world for over a thousand years. It is not because we have seen fairies with our eyes; rather, it is the product of someone's imagination."

He nodded at her explanation. The Elven Republic also had books such as she described. However, the books he read were not imaginary stories about humans. Instead, they were stories about heroic fae warriors battling monsters. He thought back to her statement about warlocks.

"In the Elven Republic, we have good warlocks and bad warlocks. The warlock housed in suspended-animation was historically one of the worst warlocks to ever inhabit our realm. He murdered fae including women and children. He was evaluated by our healers for rehab, and they determined that he could not be treated. He is the only one I have ever heard of that the healers refused to touch."

"How do you heal people with evil minds?" Stephanie asked. If the fae could do that, wouldn't it be wonderful to send them to Earth to treat all the psychopaths here? Then she thought about how humans would be diagnosed and decided that a healing skill of this sort would likely get abused.

"Talented healers can place their hands on someone's head and lift out some issues like seizures, strokes, and depression. We try to change the unhealthy brains of our fae that go bad. It keeps our prison population down. We are a long-lived people, and as you could imagine, they might spend several hundred years in prison if we operated like you humans do."

"How old are you?"

"I am about 300 years old."

"Wow." Stephanie thought about how Earth would change with longer lifespans, and it would be so overcrowded.

"Has the Elven Republic become overpopulated?"

"No. We have small families and many cities."

"Earth would be a mess if humans lived that long. We already have too many people."

"Yes."

"So, you have this bad warlock that you tried to heal into goodness, but it didn't work."

"No, the healers did not try. They can evaluate through their touch what they can and cannot fix."

"I have tomorrow off work, and I think we should visit the locations where humans have been attacked by the fae. I also want to study this grimoire to learn a few defensive spells. If we were to encounter this warlock, how would we fight him? Does he have a name?"

"His name is Ramsey. He is an elemental warlock able to harness more than one element—an exceedingly rare talent among warlocks. It is so rare that he thought he could take over the Elven Republic with it. Fortunately, he could not overcome the warriors of the court."

"Don't warlocks use wands or something like that to assist with casting their spells?"

"They do. After we captured and contained him, our people analyzed his wand and found it to be as evil as he was, so we sent it with him to the suspended-animation prison. Unfortunately, he has his greatest tool with him."

"That was very smart. I would have destroyed the wand or sent it to a different prison."

Gormon frowned at her and asked, "Are you calling the Elven Republic unintelligent?"

Stephanie thought about her assessment and nodded her head. "Example A was sending a woman to prison for over two hundred years for stealing food to feed her starving family from the royal household, and Example B was not separating an evil warlock from his most powerful weapon. Just who was making decisions at that time?"

Gormon looked at her with haughty superiority for a while before exhaling a painful grimace and admitting, "Our king was young at the time. This warlock murdered his father, and he had not expected to take over the republic for at least another hundred years. His advisors were bad, and it took him a while to sort that out. Ramsey nearly destroyed our realm and would have if not for the combined efforts of the king's warriors, mages, and other warlocks."

"Do you execute anyone in your world? Ramsey wastes the air of the Elven Republic."

"Not on purpose. We revere all living things including bad warlocks, but I do not doubt that if anyone could have single-handedly beat the warlock in a one-on-one battle, we would have chosen to dispatch him that way. An eternity in suspended-animation worked for two hundred years."

"Until humans messed that up."

"Yes."

"You're making me anxious about meeting Ramsey. What can I learn from this grimoire to have some defense against him?"

"I have not memorized that book. Let me review it. Your food was delicious. I did not recognize any of it, but it was good regardless."

"Go ahead and thank you—it's called spaghetti. I'm going to clean things up and then I'll join you." Stephanie was soon loading the dishwasher and thinking about the coming confrontation with Ramsay. She wondered if it would end her life. Then she asked herself if she really wanted to get involved. She thought about the level of evil and power that Ramsey had and knew she wanted to save Earth from this warlock. She could see him amassing an army, and with his magical abilities, taking over Earth. She was in deep to help Gormon find the dangerous warlock.

She sat at the table watching him peruse the grimoire and asked, "Why doesn't your king send you additional warriors to help in this quest to locate and contain Ramsey?"

There was a pause before Gormon answered, "Because I have not asked him."

"Why not? If it took every ally to overcome him the last time, what makes you think you can do it alone this time?"

"I have different powers on Earth. I am hoping he does also. Also, I have you and you are an unknown just yet. Besides, I need to collect the other prisoners before I get to him. Those little arrows that you have found in your patients are not coming from Ramsey."

That explanation was a lot to take in. He had some faith in her fighting abilities. Really, more faith than she had. How were his powers different on Earth? Finally, she had been so worried about Ramsey, she'd forgotten the other prisoners; and yet one or more of them had killed one human and injured others. There was lots of danger out there. She debated what to do next and decided to stay quiet while he perused the book for answers. She wasn't one to sit quietly while other people solved her problems for her, but in this situation with so much unknown to her, it was the right thing to do.

She got up to make bowls of ice cream for them, placing one in front of him with a spoon. He looked down at it and then over at her, perhaps wondering how to eat it. She dug her spoon in while grabbing a little of the caramel sauce on top, then brought the spoon to her mouth and closed her eyes in enjoyment of the dessert. When she opened them to grab a second bite, she smiled to watch Gormon deal with the sensation of something very cold touching his tongue. Apparently, they didn't have ice cream in the Elven Republic.

"What is this?"

Stephanie paused a moment to think about how to answer the question and replied, "Frozen cow's milk with caramel sauce."

"Frozen cow's milk? That does not sound delicious. What is a cow?"

"It's a large animal on Earth valued for its meat, its milk, and its hide. Do you have milk from some animal in the Elven Republic?"

"Yes, we have milk. Our herders sing to the animals for three days and then they produce milk. It has healing qualities in it, but we have never frozen it. I will have to take this product home to see if our scientists can reproduce it."

"Wouldn't it be faster to shop on Earth and portal it home?"

Gormon frowned at Stephanie's suggestion. "Your food is rumored to have lots of additives, and it would make our people sick."

"So, the Elven Republic monitors what is going on here?"

"Our worlds are connected. If you self-destruct, you will take us with you."

Stephanie wished she could deny his charge, but he was right. Then an idea came into her head. She held up her hand and said, "Just a moment."

She was soon out in her garage looking at her shelves for a box. She smiled when she saw the box and reached for it, taking it back to where the fae warrior sat.

"This is a hand-crank ice cream making machine." She briefly demonstrated it and set it aside for him to take back to his world. Having once tasted ice cream, who would want to live in a world without it? Gormon nodded and looked intrigued.

"After Ramsey, who is the next worst prisoner? Or maybe, rather than worry about the prisoners, I should master all the spells in that grimoire."

"Yes, I would rather work on your protection. There are a lot of spells in this book to learn, and I doubt you could learn more than two or three this evening."

"If you had studied in a human medical school, you would know that my memorization capacity is exceptional. I think I could handle at least ten spells as far as ingredients and words. I need time to practice the actual spell, though, which will slow me down."

Gormon looked at her and it was hard to tell what he was thinking. He usually wore a stern expression. Then she wondered if his translation charm was correctly translating from English to fae. Finally, he looked away and back down at the book.

"Since you're perusing the book, why don't you show me what spells you've found that are helpful? I'll take a picture with my phone and begin to work on them while you find more."

"Picture? Phone?"

Stephanie pulled out her phone, leaned over the open page and took a picture of it. Then she showed him the picture on her screen.

He studied the picture on her phone and said, "We have a lot of magic in the Elven Republic, but Earth has its own magic. Yes, we can go faster if I find the spells, and you practice."

Stephanie nodded and then pointed to her photo. "Is this a good one? Or was this just the page you had open?"

"Ah no, that spell is to make someone fall in love with you. I would suggest trying that tactic with Ramsey, but I cannot imagine it would work given his lack of empathy for people."

Stephanie nodded and then took a picture of the first page that Gormon thought was relevant. She looked at the page before taking the picture and asked him, "Can your translation amulet temporarily change the words from fae to English so I can take a picture? I would use Google translate, but fae is not one of the languages it has in its database."

It was clear that several of Stephanie's words did not translate. So, she took a quick side trip explaining the many spoken languages on Earth and how the software could translate.

"That is so inefficient. You must type sentences on your screen. With my amulet, I can instantly understand what you are saying. Or I can until you use some weird words from your world. However, back to your question, yes, I can make the words appear in English."

He did so for each useful spell, and she quickly snapped pictures and went to work. She was glad that a magic wand wasn't required as she didn't have one. She started small with the first spell. It would allow her to throw fire at the evil warlock. She knew she could do that only if she was in a fight to the death with him. She also didn't want to light her house on fire. So, she grabbed a candle and a coat and went into her backyard. She opened her barbecue lid and placed the candle there. Then she practiced lighting it on fire. In half an hour, she'd learned the distance and size of her effort to either light the candle or torch it. Once she had it mastered, she returned inside and thought of a new question to ask Gormon. She now could fight Ramsey with flames.

"Can Ramsey detect where you are? Does he know who you are and your role in imprisoning him two centuries ago?"

"Yes, he can detect me if I do not have my shields up, but I typically have them up at all times on Earth. As to whether he remembers my role in getting him to prison, I doubt it. There were many warriors, and I was just one. I do not believe he knows my individual signature or my role in his capture as it was extremely chaotic at the time.

Stephanie nodded and returned to studying the spells. Gormon set aside a few more to practice. She took a moment to think about her daughter off at college. What would she say if she saw her scientific-minded mother practicing magic? Did her daughter have some magic skills? She'd have to ask Gormon about it.

It was getting close to midnight and Stephanie had learned a few defensive spells. She could throw fire and put up a shield that would protect her from some things. She could move an object up to ten feet. She also learned some of Gormon's capabilities, which were by far greater than hers, but then, he had centuries of practice against her experience of little more than twenty-four hours.

"I need some sleep. It was a long day and I will need to be sharp tomorrow. Is there anything you need before I head to bed?"

He shook his head, "no." He would visit the Elven Republic to update his king, then he would meditate and spend a little time thinking about the quest ahead before this healer woke up tomorrow morning. He wondered what kind of partner she would make in the hunt for prisoners. As a warrior, he had been on many campaigns for his king, but he couldn't recall a more unusual partner than this human, nor had he had to search on Earth for the enemy before.

# Chapter Three

Stephanie was cooking a hearty breakfast. The day ahead might be the most unusual of her life. She was ignoring all of the usual things she did on a day off, like laundry, gardening, or meal prep, or even attending a favorite exercise class. Today, she was going to help Lord Warrior Gormon Mialynn re-capture some fae prisoners. She was going to assist him by using some spells she'd practiced from the grimoire. A week ago, if someone had told her she'd be using spells to help a fae warrior for the day, she would have asked what hallucinogens they were taking.

She was just finishing her breakfast when Gormon appeared in her kitchen.

"Would you like a breakfast before we set up?"

Gormon hadn't been a food person anytime during his life, but the food this healer cooked pleased his taste buds as no other fae food had. Her food gave him extra energy, as he noticed he had to meditate less to replenish his powers. He nodded his agreement and sat down, then stood up again to approach her at her countertop.

"Would you like some help?" It seemed rude to just give her his food order and then sit down waiting to be served.

She gave him a genuine smile and said, "No, I like to cook. Besides I would bet you don't know how to use a stove or perhaps how to cook the food I have in the refrigerator."

Maybe that was the problem with fae food—it was never cooked. She was correct in that he didn't know how to use the heat source that was "cooking" his food. Actually, he didn't understand any of the big machines in her kitchen. She had a big metal box that seemed to keep things cool, another machine that she put dirty dishes inside of and then they came out clean, and this hot box that she used the top or an area underneath to cook food. Normally, he would research these items, but he had been so busy traveling back and forth between worlds that he hadn't taken time to understand what she did with human food.

"You are correct—I do not know how to operate that hot box you are using at the moment. Perhaps when we are less pressed for time you can teach me. Certainly, the food you serve from the hot box has been delicious so far."

"In the human world, we call this a hot box a range and the top area is the cooktop consisting of burners that heat pans up."

"Range? I thought range was a ranch or prairie in a deserted part of your country," Gormon said, using his translation charm and trying to understand her word meanings.

Stephanie googled the answer to Gormon's question. She had never thought to ask where the name *range* originated. It was coined in the 15th century to describe a row of cooking boxes positioned in front of a fire. A cook had a range of heating options upon which to cook meals on. She explained the word to Gormon, and he nodded. He was impressed that she could find answers by pushing buttons on her *phone*. She didn't need to talk to other people to get those answers.

Stephanie brought out a map to discuss with Gormon. She was glad she still had paper maps around as everyone now used their phones to navigate. Last night she'd thought to look for one thinking it would help Gormon understand the area they would be searching for his fae prisoners. She'd put a red X where each human had been injured. She quizzed for more specifics on where the cavern was and where he'd found the fairy in the cabin. They now had five data points on the map.

"Tell me more about your prisoners and fae in general. Are you sensitive to cold? Some of these locations have snow on the ground; others don't, but the temperatures drop at night. Can your people withstand that cold?"

"Some of them can use magic to create shelter and warmth, so there is no reason for the large group of escaped prisoners to die from the cold. The fairy I came upon hiding in the cabin was not part of the big group, nor was the giant. So, one question is how many of my prisoners are tied to Ramsey's group and how many are going it alone."

"We would rather have them going it alone. It's easier to pick them off one at a time rather than facing forty-eight prisoners standing in front of Ramsey. Did you say that most of these prisoners can fly—that was how they got out of the cavern?"

Gormon nodded and studied the map while thinking about what decisions the average fae would make on Earth.

"Besides Ramsey, about what percent of the other prisoners would be willing and able to cause harm to humans?"

"Good question. I would guess at least half of Ramsey's group. There were a few errors in judgement for the sentences these prisoners received, like the fairy I met at the cabin. However, most of these prisoners were really bad fae. If the prisoners are following Ramsey, and he is the likely leader of the group, then they are doing so because they think they will get power or riches with him, or they are following out of fear of Ramsey killing them."

"I know you can portal anywhere, but let's take my car as I can't portal and we can put supplies in it. While I drive, let's go over that list that your realm prepared. Describe the fae for me —what they look like and what their powers are."

Gormon nodded and they were headed toward her garage when she stopped and asked, "Are you sensitive to cold and snow?"

He tilted his head at her with his usual haughty expression and said, "No. I have charms that keep me warm and dry."

Stephanie grabbed a parka and boots and headed into the garage mumbling, "Of course you have a charm for that."

If she had looked back, she would have seen the beginnings of a smile on her haughty warrior's face.

She backed her car out of the driveway planning to head to highway 80 toward Lake Tahoe. According to what Gormon pointed to on her map, the prison was located close to Sugar Bowl Ski Resort, and two of the injured patients came from hiking areas of the Tahoe National Forest. Patient Steckel from yesterday was in her neighborhood of Colfax, which was about fifty miles away from the prison. Colfax was a concerning location as it was the first big town exiting the Sierra Mountains. Was this Ramsey's group or lone operators?

"Gormon, I know you don't have a sense of distances on Earth, but the woman we treated yesterday morning was injured by one of your prisoners about fifty miles away from the prison. If you were strolling through the woods at a rapid pace, it would take you about thirteen hours to walk that distance. Your prisoners have been loose for about thirty-six hours and some of them can fly, so it's entirely possible to cover that distance."

She gave him a few glances while explaining the distances

and yet was still being careful to keep her eyes on the road. He nodded that he was following her explanation.

"So, two of the three injured humans have been poisoned by tiny arrows. Who on your list of fae prisoners would have those arrows and where did they get them? Surely, you didn't put the prisoners into suspended-animation with weapons?"

He grimaced, and said. "We might have done so. Again, it was an extremely chaotic time. Our king had just been murdered, and we warriors were divided between protecting the new king, holding the kingdom together, and rounding up the attackers. I know I have used the excuse of the king's murder, but there was never before a king that was assassinated or even seriously harmed by someone in our thousand-year history. All of us were in shock and we had no leadership. So yes, we sent some fae to the prison who shouldn't have gone, we gave the evil warlock his wand, and we likely so quickly moved prisoners into the prison that we did not search them for weapons before doing so. In answer to your second question about who in the Elven Republic uses those tiny arrows, it is likely a fairy. On my list of prisoners is a fairy who is a Redcap. He was sentenced after he killed several people in his village. He uses knives and arrows and he is small." Gormon held his hands apart to show how small.

Stephanie estimated the Redcap was six inches or less. "Does he have a limited number of arrows, or can he use magic to make more? Also, he's dipping these arrows in some kind of human poison. Do you know what the poison is, and does it affect people in your realm?"

Gormon liked collaborating with this woman. She was full of interesting questions and yet he sensed a moral code in her soul that would make her a friend in the Elven Republic.

"Those are good questions. He conjures his arrows with

magic and the poison he uses is charmed so it attacks people from both worlds."

"Do all fae know of Earth and humans? When your prisoners were released from suspended-animation, did they at once know they were in the human realm?"

"Yes and no. They would have immediately known they were in the human realm as it looks different from the Elven Republic, and their memories would have clicked into place as to the suspended-animation prison. What will confuse them is that the Earth they knew of at the time they entered the prison is a very different Earth than exists now. Humans still have no magic, but you have greatly advanced through technology. There were fewer people, less technology existed and you did not have these little screens that have answers to everything."

Stephanie smiled at his description of smartphones, but yes, Earth of two hundred years ago was pre-electricity, cars, computers, and the birth and death of millions of people. Even something as simple as growing food had changed, so these fae were in for some surprises. Then she thought of a question.

"If you were to get hit by a car traveling at the speed we're going right now, which is seventy miles per hour, would you survive? I mean, what kind of healing capabilities do fae have?"

Gormon looked around at vehicles traveling around them on this road and tried to imagine getting hit by one. He did not think he would survive. In fact, he didn't think even a fae giant would survive.

"If I was a fae with wings and could rise above these carriages so to avoid getting hit, then I would survive. However, even our giants, which are much larger than humans, would not survive."

"This city where the woman was attacked is close to a freeway like the one we're traveling on. So, some of your prisoners may already be dead, victims of being hit by cars or trucks," Stephanie said, pointing to an eighteen wheeler in another lane.

"True. Certainly, if you hit a four-inch fairy, it would not damage your car and you wouldn't know that you have a dead fae on the glass."

"How about Ramsey? What would happen if a car hit him going the speed I'm traveling currently?"

"He would be killed if his back was turned and he did not get out of the way. If he was facing the oncoming car, he could either stop it, put a shield up, or jump out of the way. The first two would damage or kill the occupants in the car. Has someone mentioned that happening? Did you find that story in your little box?" Gormon asked, pointing to the cell phone.

"I heard no reports on that. I was just wondering if some of your fae might already be dead, but we wouldn't know it."

"I suppose that is possible. I will check with our healers back in the realm to see if they have any ideas. Maybe we can send someone to this area who can sense magic residue that would point to the death of a fae. Of course, they likely would not be able to identify which prisoner was on someone's carriage glass."

"Cars and trucks. *Carriages* in our world refers to something pulled by a horse. I'm driving a car and those are trucks," Stephanie said, point to both pick-up trucks and eighteen-wheel trucks.

"Cars and trucks," Gormon repeated. As part of his translation charm, he could attach pictures to words, and he did so with what his eyes were seeing on this road.

"Do you have mountains in the Elven Republic?"

"Not as tall as your mountains seem to be, but our world is not flat."

"We'll arrive at the location of yesterday's attack soon. Do you have any way to sense the Redcap fairy? How do we find him?"

"The Redcap is a shapeshifter, so I cannot give you a description of his appearance. I have the ability to sense magic at all times, but I do not know how to explain my range."

"In about ninety minutes, we've traveled eighty Earth miles. Could that distance be your range?" Stephanie asked, trying to think of ways to explain distances.

Gormon thought about his answer and said, "Perhaps half that distance. I a m sensing magic the closer we get to this city you called Colfax."

"Can you pinpoint the source of the magic?"

"I should be able to, yes."

"Do you want me to park, or do you want me to drive closer to your source of magic?"

"I think you should park and then I will use my charm to keep us both invisible as we approach the source of the magic. Given the Redcap's shapeshifter ability, I would rather see him or her before they see us."

Okay, Stephanie thought, this is all getting very real. As she searched for a parking space, she was reviewing in her mind the spells she had learned from the grimoire. They were surrounded by forest; how were they ever going to find a shapeshifter? She parked, got out of the car and locked it, and looked over at Gormon. He had swords scabbarded on his back. He walked around the car to her, but then disappeared.

"Where did you go?" she whispered and then she jumped when something touched her.

"I am here, but invisible. I am going to grab your hand and hold onto it. This will extend my charm to you and tell you which direction we are walking."

"Okay. How will you know your charm is working?"

"I will not be able to see you, just feel your hand; and if we look for our images in your car's mirrors, we will not see anything."

"Okay."

Stephanie found that she was strolling toward the woods walking hand in hand with Gormon. His hand was callused, perhaps from sword practice, or just three centuries of living. For all the perfect features of the elf, his hands showed the imperfections of that life.

He stopped and whispered, "We are getting close to the source. Walk quietly and be careful where you step—we do not want to alert anyone by sounding like a giant tromping through the woods. Keep your eyes open and tug my hand if you see something, and I will do likewise. We can point to a spot on our palms where we see an unusual object. My plan is to create a portal and send him or her back to the realm. To do so, I will have to let go of your hand. I will place your hand on my waist, and you will need to keep it there as I move to stay invisible. Understand?"

"Yes," she whispered back wishing, he'd given these instructions before they got close to the source of magic.

They continued forward and she was looking all around—above in the trees, on the ground, and to the sides. She caught a glimpse of something to her side and blinked to focus. Then she tugged on Gormon's hand.

They stopped and as he suggested, she held out her palm and moved his hand to where she saw something. After checking her hand to verify the finger position, she turned her eyes to where she spotted something unusual. She was gratified to see that it was still there. Was it a problem with her eyesight or was this the Redcap?

# Chapter Four

She soon found her hand on Gormon's waist as he approached the spot where they both saw something suspicious. Before she had the chance to keep up to his pace, she lost touch with him and froze, continuing to stare at the potential Redcap. He surged toward her and then the air in front of her shimmered and she couldn't see him.

She startled when Gormon appeared right in front of her. "What just happened?"

"You found the Redcap, then when you let go of me, he could see you and went on the attack. So, I set up a portal and he is now causing problems back on the Elven Republic."

"So, we're down to 47 or so prisoners?"

"Yes."

"Do you detect any more magic nearby?" Stephanie asked. She was tempted to sniff the air, but knew she couldn't smell magic.

She watched him as he seemed to stretch out his senses and rotate around.

"I detect faint magic that way," he said, pointing northeast toward Lake Tahoe.

"What does that mean? Can you detect magic in me? I want to learn to detect it."

"Remember, I grew up in the Elven Republic and learned how to detect magic at an early age."

"You're never too old to learn. You need to teach me. What will happen to me and Earth if you die in battle or must return to your realm?"

"I will not die in battle or leave you alone to battle the prisoners," Gormon replied haughtily.

Oh my gosh, she'd put his back up with that comment.

"So, you've never been seriously injured in battle? How long do elves live?"

"Yes, I have needed the services of a healer, but I have always healed quickly. I have at least another seven centuries ahead of me."

"If you get injured on Earth, I'm your only healer and I'm not as powerful as you are at healing. Should you ask a healer from your world to come here in case you have an early battle with Ramsey?"

Again, he turned his stare on her as if that was the dumbest idea ever, but then his shoulders relaxed and he said, "You may have a point. I am the best weapon against Ramsey, but I may need some healing along the way."

"Were you injured during your last battle with Ramsey?"

Again, he sighed and lifted his shirt to show a long jagged scar from his tummy to his side. Stephanie stared at it and knew she didn't want to help treat Gormon out in the middle of nowhere for an injury of that size.

"Yes, bring a healer here. I have some stuff in my car to treat a wound like that, but depending on how deep it went, you might die before you reached the hospital. How come you have a scar? I though your healing abilities prevented your skin from scarring. At least, that is what happens in fantasy stories in the human realm."

"I asked the healer not to heal that scar. I wanted to remember that time in our fae history and the treachery that can be done by unsuspecting fae."

"Oh."

"Back to your question about sensing magic. You are not a fae; rather, you are a human who is in the process of acquiring the ability to do spells. Therefore, you are unlikely to have the ability to sense magic."

"Still, tell me how you sense magic in case I someday get that feeling. Maybe I'm not 100% human. Maybe I'm mixed with a fae and that is what has given me the ability to cast spells."

He looked at her with an air of superiority that only elves could master. It was the carved face, muscled body, and pointed ears that all managed to say, "You are an inferior human," without his uttering a word. So, she shrugged and laughed at herself and the situation she found herself in. Then she closed her eyes and tried to sense the world around her. She heard leaves rustling, a woodpecker hammering on a tree, and other noises of the forest. Did she feel magic? No. So she opened her eyes to find Gormon staring at her and asked, "Where to next?"

Gormon put his hand in the air and pointed in the general direction of Lake Tahoe. "I have a faint sense of magic in that direction."

"Can you tell if it is more than one prisoner?"

"Yes. I am sensing only one fae."

They walked back to her car, and she returned to a discussion about other missing prisoners.

"Was the fae you portaled back to your realm the only

Redcap on your list of prisoners? Also, do you have any theory as to why he was by himself and so far away from perhaps a larger group of prisoners?"

"He was the only Redcap on the list, so you should not see any more humans attacked with tiny arrows. Ramsey is a persuasive leader. I would guess half of the fae following him are doing so as they agree with his vision of taking over this world. The other half are afraid of his power and are following out of fear."

"I know Ramsey nearly took over your world, but he'll never take over this world. It will take him too long to understand our technology. We have weapons of mass destruction that we would drop on him the moment he proves to be a challenge to the human world. He can't magic away a nuclear bomb."

"I do not understand your terms of *weapons of mass destruction or nuclear bombs*, but I think you are correct that like the warriors from the Elven Republic, the warriors of this world would collectively defeat him."

"You should read our history of World War II to understand the warrior capabilities of this world. The technology is old as it happened around eighty years ago, but it's a good reflection of who we are."

They entered her car and Stephanie smiled as she saw Gormon automatically put on his seatbelt. He must understand the physics of a speeding car in an accident. She pulled out a paper map to discuss where exactly they were heading. He pointed to a place on the map and said, "This is our next source of magic. I suspect it is another fairy. The fairies are loners and the least likely to join Ramsey. Also, they're small and can fly and can quietly get away from him."

"So, what kind of fairies are on your prisoner list? Do you know what they were sentenced for so we can understand if they are a wrongfully detained prisoner or a real threat to us?"

"I think it is likely that there are only two other prisoners on my list that will be set free. I do have what their crimes were, and none seem as minor as stealing food from the royal household like the first fairy's story."

"What's your justice system like? Do the fae get a fair trial?"

"What do you mean by a fair trial?"

"When you are accused, is there someone that defends you? What kind of evidence is required? Is there a group of peers who listen to your side of the story to determine if you should be convicted and sent to prison?"

"No. We simply mind-scour anyone accused of a crime for the truth. We do have a committee that reads the results of that scour to determine if the fae is guilty."

Stephanie whipped her head around at that statement. Wait, he could read minds? Was he constantly hearing her thoughts? How close did he have to be to mind-scour someone. Did that hurt your head? How did you get into someone's head and look at just their relevant thoughts? She turned off her car's engine, needing to hear more about this.

Stephanie looked over at Gormon and said, "You better explain this mind scour thing to me. From my perspective as a human, it sounds terrible."

Gormon studied her and must have realized she was upset. So, he started at the beginning.

"In the Elven Republic about half of the time, we do not talk out loud to our friends and family. We talk by sharing our thoughts with each other."

"How do you share your thoughts?" Stephanie asked. This might be one concept too strange for her to grasp.

"We look at each other and transmit our thoughts. I can

only receive the thoughts of the person I'm looking at—I cannot walk up to a group of people and hear all of their thoughts at once."

"Have you used that technique to mind-scour me?"

"No. It does not seem to work on humans."

Stephanie heaved a sigh of relief at that comment, glad there was something he couldn't do.

"Can someone hide their thoughts from you or hold onto a vision of someone else committing a crime? How accurate is this mind-scour thing?"

"Ramsey was able to do as much damage as he did to the kingdom because he was talented at diverting the mind-scour. He was able to hold an image in his mind that gave a false picture of his true thoughts. As far as I can remember, he is the only fae that has been able to avoid the mind-scour process."

"When you caught him, how were you able to send him to prison without proof from a mind-scour?"

"We had witnesses to his action."

"In our justice system, you need evidence that someone has committed a crime. We assign a lawyer to represent the accused and another lawyer represents the government to give evidence and convince twelve random people that you are guilty."

"That sounds like a slow process. In the Elven Republic, we can decide who a criminal is in a short period of time."

"Can every fae scour a mind, or is this the skill of just some of your people?"

"The ability to mind-scour is a skill unique to elves, and not all elves can do it. I do not have that skill. Fairies, giants, and warlocks do not have this ability."

Stephanie felt relieved knowing he hadn't been able to read her mind when she was thinking about how handsome he was —that would be embarrassing. She started the engine and headed back onto the highway in search of the next magic signal.

"What kind of fairy are we looking for this time?"

"I think it is a banshee. She was sent to prison for murder. She'll be bigger than a redcoat, but smaller than you."

Stephanie combed her memory for a banshee description and asked, "They're always female and don't they make ships crash or something?"

"That tale is not correct. Banshees wail or scream outside of the house where a death is about to occur. This banshee turned out to be inaccurate and so people were rude and tried to make her go away. In retaliation, she began hastening the death of anyone who annoyed her. It improved her accuracy, and people were no longer rude, but then her behavior was suspicious, and she was mind-scoured and we found that she was poisoning people."

"She can't do anything to me as long as I don't take her poison, correct?"

"Correct. She should be easy to portal back to my realm."

As Gormon predicted, she was easy to capture and send back to the Elven Republic. Now they were on the hunt for one more lone magic signal, and then they would return to Stephanie's home. It had been a long day, and her head was filled with all kinds of new knowledge about Gormon's world. This next fae was likely to be much trickier than the first two. Gormon was sensing a half-elf. There were a few half-elves on his prisoner list, and he couldn't sense which one was ahead. He thought it was likely a male who was sentenced for being a part of the plot to overthrow the fae kingdom. That male was known to be a loner and wasn't originally connected to Ramsey's group. The half-elf he had in mind was known as Michael, as half-elves were not given elven names. The Elven Republic regarded them poorly, Michael was unhappy as a half-elf. His mother, a human, has died while he was in prison, and his father didn't really know what to do with a half-elf while he was growing up, so he was not much help to Michael when he was bullied.

"The next magic signal that we are following is likely a half-elf by the name of Michael. There are three half-elves on the list, but Michael is known for being a loner. In his mind he had much to be unhappy about. The King's disdain for half-elves was well known in the realm, and Michael was convicted and imprisoned for trying to overthrow the king. He will likely sense me coming. He is a good fighter and certainly has no reason to want to return to the Elven Republic."

"Could he stay in the human world and be a healer?"

Gormon sighed, understanding where the doctor's question came from. However, he was sure that Michael had too much resentment to be happy and productive in the human realm.

"We can ask, but I doubt he would be interested in healing."

"Let me talk to him and see if I can convince him. Would your realm release him to Earth if he agreed to become a healer here?"

"That is a complicated question. How would you manage his healer skills? I witnessed many needs in your hospital. That was just one hospital of many in your city, and there are many cities in the world. Who gets healed by Michael?"

"Fair question. I don't have the answer to that. Do we assign him to heal children or mothers of young children, or some other population? What happens to Earth once we begin healing people in mass numbers? Is there food and housing for those extra people who otherwise would have died in the normal course of events? Are we acting as a supreme being who decides who gets to live or die? We already do that in many parts of this world, as some countries have better healthcare than others. There are so many ethical questions, that as much as I would love the healer touch in this world, we don't have the structure to use it wisely. So, let's not offer Michael that option."

Gormon was impressed that she could reason through using a magical skill in her world, especially as she was a healer as well. Then she asked another thoughtful question.

"Would you give him a pardon in your world if he served as your healer to care for any injuries we incur as we confront other prisoners and eventually Ramsey? I think Ramsey is likely the last prisoner we'll confront as he'll sacrifice all the prisoners before him."

"That is a good question. Let me talk with my king and I will be back. With that, he opened a portal in front of him without thinking it through, and before he realized his mistake, the car and Stephanie were in the Elven Republic. Whoops.

# Chapter Five

Stephanie found herself sitting in her car in a world she didn't recognize. She looked around and found they were in the courtyard of what appeared to be a castle, or at least a castle in her world. There were other elves in the courtyard staring at her and Gormon seated inside the car. Some had swords in hand ready to do battle.

"I am sorry about this. I did not think through opening a portal where I did. Welcome to the Elven Republic."

Gormon opened the door and got out, saying something to the others in the courtyard in a language she didn't understand. She opened her door and got out of her car. Her immediate thought was, could she breathe the air in this alternative reality? Then she remembered that Michael was half-human and half fae, so she should be good to go. She stared around at the beautiful men and women inside this courtyard, relieved to see them relaxing the swords in their hands. She didn't want to die here—what about her daughter on Earth? What about her job and a thousand other things? Still, a tiny part of her mind was excited to be here—in a place few humans had ever visited. In fact, she didn't see any humans here in the courtyard.

Stephanie approached Gormon and said, "What do I do now? How do we get back home?"

He looked down at her as though he expected a better question from her than how she was to return home.

"You can remain by your car in the courtyard while I have a brief conversation with my king, then we will portal back to Earth."

"We can't just return to the highway; we'll cause an accident."

"I will return us to a parking lot or your house. We will be safe," he insisted and turned to walk toward an entrance.

"Wait! Your kin have swords in their hands. I'll join you on your visit with your king."

"You will be safe here. I told them that you were not a threat."

"Then why haven't they sheathed their swords? No thanks, I'm not staying here alone."

Gormon looked around and saw she was correct. His kin were not pointing their swords at her, but they had not put their weapons away. Among the kin were an ex-mate of his. Granted they had not dated in over a decade, but she was vindictive, which was one of the reasons they were no longer together. Perhaps Stephanie was correct, and the courtyard was not safe for her. He sighed and nodded, and she quickly closed the gap to him.

Stephanie followed him inside a door and up a set of stone stairs to another level of the building. It looked like a reception area as it was large and well decorated in terms of fabrics and plants. Gormon approached a guard at the far end of the room and said something in his language. The guard nodded and disappeared behind a closed door.

Gormon turned away from the door and directed Stephanie to a seating area. He remained standing at attention. The silence in the large room stretched to an uncomfortable length. Stephanie had pinched herself to see if it caused pain. Perhaps this was a dream, and she really wasn't in another realm, but the pinch hurt.

The door opened and Gormon somehow straightened to even more rigid attention and then he bowed from the neck and said, "Sire."

Stephanie stood up from her chair and catalogued the man approaching her. He was as beautiful as Gormon, if not more so. His clothes were similar to Gormon's, though he carried no swords in sheaths on his back. He may be a king, but he wasn't her king, so she held out her hand and said, "Hello Sir, I'm Dr. Stephanie Jones and I've accidentally ended up in your kingdom."

He briefly grasped her hand and replied, "So I have heard from Lord Mialynn. I also understand there is an automobile as I believe you call it in my courtyard. I hope it still works as the goblins in this realm are likely studying it right now."

Stephanie gasped and ran over to the window and was pleased to see that her car was untouched. It was relatively new and worth at least thirty thousand dollars on Earth. She didn't want the goblins dismantling it for parts.

She looked back at the king and saw a brief smile as he said, "Do not worry, I will not let anyone near it."

"Thank you, and thank you for translating your language into mine. I appreciate your sending Gormon to Earth. The prisoners have caused some illnesses and death among humans, and without his help and that of your other warriors, we would have more problems on Earth. Thankfully, it's been contained, and no one in the human world knows that fae prisoners are on the loose. We've found two and returned them to this world, and we have a question about a third," Stephanie said, looking over at Gormon to finish the story.

"Sire," Gormon said, continuing in English so Stephanie could understand. "We are close to contacting Michael. If you will recall, he is the half-elf half-human and has resented the Elven Republic for treating him differently given his mixed heritage. He wanted your father dead as he had some negative thoughts about mixed heritage and not because he was a follower of Ramsey. Dr. Jones pleaded for him to be left on Earth as a healer but recognized the moral issues with doing that. What are your thoughts about Michael?"

Stephanie was amazed that this king might know the stories of all the prisoners who were released on Earth.

"He and I are of a similar age, and I remember the merciless bullying he underwent as a result of my father's attitude toward mixed-heritage fae. I wonder how my father would feel today if he saw just how many mixed-heritage beings there are in this world. Thankfully, his attitude is not the attitude of the moment. I am willing to grant him amnesty as long as he has no plans to kill me. I would recommend that he not be allowed to stay in the human realm. His powers could lead to abuse."

"I don't know how travel by portal works, but what is to stop your fae from deciding to come to Earth and create havoc?" Stephanie asked.

"It's against the code of this kingdom to intervene in another world. Furthermore, most fae lack a portal skill."

"Does Michael have a portal skill?" Stephanie asked.

Gormon and the king looked at each other and then the king said, "I don't know."

"Do you keep records on fae lineage and special abilities?"

"They may be kept by the schools. I'll ask our head of schools if they have such records," the king said, and he turned and left the room.

Gormon looked at Stephanie and said, "Let's return to your automobile and then we will portal back to your world."

As they walked through the castle she asked, "Is the time the same in your world as it is on Earth?"

He looked puzzled by her question, so she added, "My watch says that an hour has passed. Since my watch is connected to my phone and there are no cell towers here, I presume it is keeping time by Earth standards. If we return to Earth and my watch is correct, we'll have about thirty minutes to find Michael before sunset, when my world will begin to darken. I would rather not search for prisoners in the dark."

"I think we are okay. I will portal us back to an area that is close to Michael and safe for your car. I will do a trial run before moving you and the car."

Stephanie was relieved. She could envision so many bad scenarios with her car ending up back on Earth atop a tree or being hit by a large cargo truck. They returned to her car, and she watched as Gormon opened a portal and disappeared. She knew she should be enjoying her time in an alternative universe, but all she could think of was problems back on Earth and the physics of getting her car and herself back. She was running through a few doomsday scenarios of her travel when Gormon reappeared.

"I have a good place to land on Earth. Can you start your car and have it move forward slowly across the courtyard and I will see if I can portal us back to Earth."

There were a lot of maybes in that scenario, but at least both of them were healers, Stephanie thought as she started the car. Other fae in the courtyard stared with curiosity at the moving car and then they were out of her sight as they traveled back to Earth. The moment she saw pine trees, she hit the brake pedal hard, jerking them against their seatbelts.

"Whew! We made it safely back home. Give me a moment and I'll follow your directions of where we need to go."

Stephanie took deep breaths and pinched herself again just to make sure this wasn't a dream. She didn't think it was, as her dreams were never this clear. Usually, dreams were fuzzy rather than in high-definition.

"Why do you keep pinching yourself?" Gormon asked. "I do not recall that being a spell in the grimoire."

Stephanie smiled at him and said, "It's something that humans do to make sure they're awake and not in a dream. You have to admit for a human, my world has been turned upside down over the last few days—not only as a human, but as physician and a scientist. Though to be fair, most of my dreams involve being late for a test, a lecture, or a flight. Do elves dream?"

Gormon stared at her, puzzled at her answer, "Our dreams are not like yours, apparently. We avoid dreams as they are fantasy and lies."

"Actually, that sounds like human dreams. My dreams are a lie as I've never missed a test, an interview, or a flight, but it seems to be one of my greatest fears, so it's a regular feature in my dreams."

"Hmm, our dreams are more chaotic than that as we live centuries longer than humans. We do not sleep like humans; rather, we meditate and avoid dreaming if we can."

"Wow, I hadn't thought of that," Stephanie said, trying to imagine what three hundred years of missing tests would be like. "Usually, I envy you your long lives, but when it comes to dreams, I'm happy for the shorter human lifespan, I think."

Gormon nodded and held up his hand to the direction he wanted her to drive. He'd noted that she seemed more relaxed than when she initially came through the portal. He understood some of her angst given how much the car weighed and how fast it moved. Stephanie directed the car in that direction as Gormon said, "We are close to the magic signal that I think is Michael, but I might be wrong."

Stephanie parked along the side of the road and they got out of the car.

"Same plan as with the last two?"

Gormon nodded, taking her hand as they both disappeared from view. He led the way into the woods as they looked around. Stephanie jumped when Gormon whispered, "I think Michael is also using an invisibility charm. I can sense him in this area, but I cannot see him."

"Okay. I'll give it a try."

She let go of Gormon hand and called out, "Michael? Are you in this forest? I've spoken with the elven king, and we would like to discuss options." She figured that since he was half-human, he likely spoke English. She walked over to sit on a log and waited for something to happen.

"We?"

She heard a voice nearby and turned her head that way but couldn't see anything or anyone.

"Your king, Lord Warrior Gormon Mialynn, and I."

Suddenly, she felt an arm come around her neck and reacted on instinct. She bent over the log and tried to throw whatever body was attached to the arm around her neck. She heard a grunt as something hit the forest floor. Gormon turned off his charm and she was relieved she could see him. He also did something with Michael's charm, as soon he was visible too, though lying on the ground.

"After spending two centuries in suspended-animation, I am a little weak. Otherwise, you would have never had the upper hand on me."

"That is probably true," Gormon said, offering the man a hand up.

The man took a few moments and then accepted the proffered hand. He then took a seat on a log near Stephanie and asked, "What now?"

"We need to chat," Stephanie replied.

"Who are you?" Michael asked.

"I'm Dr. Stephanie Jones, an emergency department physician, or healer in your world. You're on Earth and you spent two hundred years in suspended animation."

Michael shook his head at the waste of his life for the past two hundred years. He looked over at the elf and raised an eyebrow in question.

"I'm Lord Warrior Gormon Mialynn of the Elf King's detail. My current mission is to recapture the forty-seven or so prisoners from the Elven Republic now loose on Earth. Dr. Jones is my human partner in this endeavor."

"Who is the Elf King?" Michael asked with a frown.

"King Kanruil, the son of the king you wanted dead," Gormon replied, which was good since Stephanie was never introduced to the man on their short visit.

"So, his father must be dead. Good riddance. Now King Kanruil wants to send me to a new prison."

"It depends," Stephanie replied.

"Are you interested in killing King Kanruil?" Gormon asked.

"Is he the same bully his father is? I suppose I am still considered worthless as a half-elf."

"Actually, times have changed and there are many fae in the kingdom who are mixed breeds. The prejudice of King Kanruil's father is gone except for a few pockets of people of his age. You are no longer unique," Gormon said.

"I suppose my mother is gone, but do you know if my father is alive?" Michael asked.

"I asked that question while recently in the realm, and your father is alive and you have siblings."

"Siblings? I remember a sister. Is there more than one?"

"Yes, although I do not know who they are or if your father remarried."

Michael had a lot to think about. The prior king was absolutely hateful toward half-elves, and he had tolerated years of bullying and death threats over it. His sister had fared better as she was younger and female. He'd reached his breaking point and during a time of turmoil in the Elven Republic decided that the king needed to be gone. Before he had achieved his goal someone else had done it for him, but the thoughts were in his head and the elven mind-readers sensed his thoughts and sentenced him to the endless prison. Now it seemed he had a chance to start over.

"What do you think I should do?" Michael asked Gormon.

"Let me answer that question," Stephanie said, butting in. "We have over forty prisoners to round up here on Earth culminating with the capture of Ramsey, the evil and powerful warlock who did succeed in killing the prior king. We could use your help in this mission as you have some healing ability. On Earth, we give people medicine, or we cut their bodies open to fix stuff. If Gormon is injured by one of the prisoners, my method of healing is slower. Also, by spending time with us, you can slowly acclimate to the new world that is Earth and the Elven Republic, which should make your decision making easier."

Michael hadn't made it past one of Stephanie's sentences. "Wait, you cut people open? Do humans die from that?"

"I saw it for myself—the inside of the human body—and I hope to never see it again, but it did work," Gormon said.

Michael was having one shocking revelation after another

after he'd been released from prison. He remembered rumors about Ramsey who was doing his best to organize the prisoners. He waited until he was behind a few other prisoners before he tried his teleportation skill to get out of the cavern. It worked and he moved away from the mountain top as fast as he could. He didn't recognize this world as it was not the Earth of when he entered the prison. He was confused as to what he should do next. The only decision he'd been able to make was to get away from Ramsey. He sensed the approach of the fae and someone else and remembered how do to an invisibility charm. It was time to take control of his life.

"I will do as the human suggests and help you round up the other prisoners. I hope you will reconsider the sentences of some of them as I think they were unfairly judged."

"We already have. We have found a fairy who stole food from the royal household to feed her starving family has been released and reunited with her family. You will be our second prisoner who is released, and there may be more. The other warriors and I returned about half the prisoners to the realm, and each case is being evaluated. However, some of the prisoners are harming or killing humans, and that is a quick trip back to the Elven Republic and a new prison. We have already returned a Redcap and a Banshee today. I will let the king know that you have joined our team, have no plans to kill him, and would like to be reunited with your family after we are done here. Okay?"

Michael put his hand over his heart and nodded, and Gormon likewise did the same. Stephanie thought this must be some fae promise or commitment gesture. She turned her back on the two men and said, "Let's return to my car and head home."

There was silence behind her as they followed her back to the car. She suspected the two men were talking telepathically with perhaps Gormon explaining what Michael should expect in this world.

They approached her car, and Stephanie opened the back door for Michael to get in. She then showed him how to apply his seatbelt and they were off.

# Chapter Six

Stephanie grabbed a pizza on the way home. Gormon looked horrified by the junk food, but Michael was excited to try real food. He ate several slices while looking around her home. She showed him how water and electricity worked as well as the indoor plumbing. She was glad he had Gormon to aid with his re-entry to the Elven Republic.

She pulled out the paper maps and the three of them discussed the remaining prisoners and where they might be, and what special abilities they had. Gormon also took a moment to work with Michael on his abilities given that they had remained unused for two centuries. They also discussed Stephanie's new and growing witch abilities and her work schedule. She was supposed to return to work the next day, but she was debating taking time off, switching to the night shift, or working as planned and being on the lookout for injuries potentially caused by a fae prisoner.

Stephanie had Gormon write down the list of prisoners for her, as he was carrying it around in his head, which was of little help to her but made sense for him as elves spoke telepathically.

"I think we should go after the low-lying fruit as we say on Earth—the prisoners with weak powers or those for whom the Elven Republic may want to reconsider their sentence. Michael, in your brief time loose on Earth, did you interact with anyone on this list? Either in the cavern after you were all released or anyone since as you have wandered this forest"

Michael studied the list and considered his brief interactions. "There's only one person on this list that I remember any contact in the cavern. He was young at the time of his imprisonment and seemed totally lost. His crime according to your list was also stealing food to feed his family. Maybe we could go down this list and recommend the release of any prisoner who stole food or had another, non-violent charge. Is it possible to reach back to the current king for amnesty for anyone with a non-violent charge? I think two centuries of time in prison is more than enough."

"Yes, I agree with you, Michael. On Earth, people get a life sentence for violent offenses like multiple murders. A single murder might get you twenty to thirty years in prison, but then, our average life expectancy is perhaps eighty years, and prisoners often have poor health due to their diet, lack of exercise, violence in our prisons, and age. In many parts of this world, people who steal food rarely go to jail as they haven't hit a monetary threshold to be prosecuted."

"King Kanruil has changed our justice system, and the only reason the suspended-animation prison was not fixed was because people forgot about it. Also, Ramsey was known to be there, and no one wanted him released," Gormon said. "As to your work schedule, why don't you go to work as scheduled the next few days to see if anyone arrives with suspected injuries from a prisoner? Michael and I can portal into the mountains and handle some of these prisoners. We could then stop by your work and heal anyone needing our help. If you have an emergency with a patient harmed by the fae, you can text me and I will portal into the hospital and help."

"I thought your Earth system worked on medicines and cutting bodies open. What can I do?" asked Michael.

"Gormon was helpful yesterday as he could counteract a poison applied to an arrow shot by a Redcap that was deadly to humans. I think he also dealt with injuries from a shapeshifter. Then, for the grand finale, he went to the children's area and healed the kids."

"Oh, okay. Can we speak to you through your mind?"

"No. We use something called cellular phones to talk and text. I got Gormon a device and I'll get you one as well. The cool thing about our technology is that you can be some distance away and yet still talk to Gormon or me. I assume there's a distance limit of your telepathic conversations; otherwise, wouldn't you hear hundreds of voices at once?" Stephanie said.

"This is true. We must be close to each other to talk. When King Kanruil wants to speak with me, I must return to the Elven Republic for that conversation," Gormon said.

"How does he get a message to you that he wants to chat?" Stephanie asked. At times when trying to understand the fae world, she felt like her head was going to explode thinking about the ways that the Elven Republic was different from Earth.

"The king has a way of projecting his need for a conversation. I do not hear his voice; rather, I just get this feeling that he wants to speak to me."

"It sounds like your king has special powers for communication," Stephanie said.

"Yes. Throughout our history, our kings have bonded with

us. I do not understand what the skill is; I only know that it works."

When Stephanie had purchased a phone for Gormon, she acquired a second one at the same time, in case his phone got damaged. She retrieved that second phone for Michael and gave him instructions on how to use it. They would have to talk in English, however, as the elven language wasn't a choice. They returned to a map of the area to plot where Gormon and Michael should search. Then she thought of another question.

"Michael, can you open a portal to the Elven Republic?" Stephanie felt stupid asking this question as she didn't even understand how portals worked. Then, before Michael could answer, she asked a second question of him: "Do you have all the powers that Gormon does? If you're a half-elf, do you have half the magical power of a full elf?"

"I can't open a portal mostly because I was never trained. I probably could learn. With time and training, I should have the same abilities as Gormon. Why?"

"If you or Gormon is injured doing battle with a prisoner, can the other person portal both of you to the Elven Republic for treatment?"

"With the exception of Ramsey, there is no one on this prisoner list who should be able to seriously injure me," Gormon said.

Stephanie could tell she had insulted Gormon's warrior abilities with the question, but she didn't care. She wanted to know that they would be safe while chasing these prisoners. While she wasn't a warrior herself, she did have the ability to treat injuries, and she knew Earth and where she could get help.

"I wish I had some way to communicate with your world when I need help in this world," Stephanie said. "Could your king send someone here whose sole purpose is to speak between the two worlds?"

Gormon sighed and replied, "One of the principles of our realm is not to change your world. Our presence here and that of the prisoners is changing the course of life here. We are trying to quietly remove our prisoners to have as little impact as possible. Can you imagine how your world would react if it knew there were magical beings here? Looking back in your history, approximately three hundred years ago, your people burned and drowned witches. Power-hungry humans would try to capture you if they knew you were an extraordinary human. This is the worry of our king."

Stephanie realized this was the missing piece of the story that she hadn't understood. From the beginning, she had wondered why Gormon didn't have more help. He was one warrior trying to collect nearly fifty fae prisoners. The Elven Republic had loads of beings who could help him, but now she understood the king's caution—he was doing his utmost not to change the course of history on Earth as well as keep the Elven Republic hidden.

"You must make sure you do not get injured here. If you do, I will do everything in my medical training to make sure you live. If I need to cut you open to heal wounds and my people see your ears and whatever is different on the inside of you, then that will happen. Maybe I can sell you as a friend who loved Star Trek so much that he had his ears surgically modified to be like Spock. Are elven bodies different on the inside than those of humans?"

Both Gormon and Michael shuddered at her comments, but Michael asked, "Star Trek? Spock? Cut me open?"

Stephanie spent a few minutes finding an episode of the classic show and explained it to her fae friends.

They were amazed about the technology and entertainment and how relatively close the show's character of Spock was to elves. She downloaded a full season to their phones so they could watch when they had time.

"This is such a strange world. You have all this technology, but no magic. You have plays with elves in them, but your people do not believe we are real. Though to be fair, the only thing that makes that character called Spock look like an elf is his ears. His coloring and haircut are all wrong," Michael said.

"In my short experience with you and Gormon, you seem to have a similar personality to Spock. I do agree, given my short visit to your realm, that Spock doesn't look like an elf."

"You've visited the Elven Republic?" Michael asked, surprise in his voice.

"It was a mistake on Gormon's part. He opened a portal while we were traveling down a freeway and the entire car with me in it landed on the palace grounds."

"I wish I was there to watch that. Did you meet the king?"

"I did, but we were there for only a short period of time. He seemed reasonable. It's getting late, so I'm going to head to bed to sleep. You guys can watch more Star Trek episodes or meditate or whatever. Good luck tomorrow," Stephanie said, getting ready to head to bed. It had been a long day. She wasn't intellectually working hard, but her world had been turned upside down and coping with these changes was taxing. She hoped that the elves were not overly confident in their abilities to capture these prisoners. She was very worried about them. She thought they were too confident in their own abilities. A few moments later, the house was quiet and she sank into sleep.

Her alarm went off after what felt like too little sleep, but she dressed in scrubs for the day ahead. She was in her kitchen fixing a breakfast of eggs, toast, and coffee when Gormon and Michael entered her kitchen. She offered to make them breakfast, which they accepted. She left the dishes in the sink to deal with when she returned home, wished them good luck, and grabbed her purse to head to the garage. She was shortly in the crowded morning commute to work. Wouldn't it be wonderful if humans could portal everywhere instead of wasting their lives in traffic?

She walked into the emergency department a few minutes before the start of her shift. She put her purse and coat in a locker and grabbed a clean white coat to put on over her scrubs. Scrubs were boring to wear day after day, but she'd ruined more than one set of street clothes with some poor patient's bodily fluids. She received a report from her colleague who was finishing up her shift. None of the patients sounded like they had injuries from a fae prisoner. She hoped the day continued that way.

The shift started out with the usual accidents, chest pain, diabetic reactions, and child fevers. Generally, it was quiet at the start of the day shift, and the number of patients increased after lunchtime. She was pleased to get a text from Gormon relaying the uneventful capture of another of the prisoners halfway through the morning. Then a patient arrived in severe mental distress and it took several people to control the man before they were able to give him sedation and call for a psych consult. She ended up treating one of the staff for an injury they incurred in dealing with the violent man. She felt her phone vibrate, but it took her some time to pull it out of her coat pocket to see who was texting her. Her heart dropped when she saw that it was a second message from Gormon.

They had encountered an Aboleth in Lake Tahoe, and Michael and Gormon were injured. He was portaling them back to the Elven Republic and would be out of touch. Stephanie had to do a search to find out what an Aboleth was. Her message from Gormon was so inadequate. What were their injuries? How long would it take them to heal? Did they capture the Aboleth or was it still lurking in Lake Tahoe? She replied with a text asking for more information, but she knew she wouldn't be getting answers anytime soon.

Then she made a possible connection. The patient they had to subdue earlier was transported from the Lake Tahoe area. What if this patient encountered the Aboleth? It sounded like this creature took over the mind of people that got in its way along with other horrid things. She pulled up a file from her phone. It was the grimoire that she saved. She searched for information about this fae, and the more she read the more worried she became. She could cleave the head off, and the body would reproduce. Did she have a spell that would work on the creature and what about the patient in her hospital? If she told anyone he was under the control of a fae creature called an Aboleth, they would get a psych consult for her. Before she could finish her search, another patient arrived needing her care. Her shift continued in that manner with rare breaks until her colleagues arrived to take over.

Once she returned home, she had two tasks on her list: Find out if she had a spell that could deal with the creature and look up every other creature on the prisoner list to find out more about them. The spells were not creature-specific, rather, she could create amulets and talismans, or use charms and spells to raise creatures. What would happen if she found a spell that would cause the Aboleth to come out onto dry land, or in the case of Lake Tahoe, snow-covered land? Would it die without water to immerse itself in? It was worth a try. With her fae friends laid up in another world, and humans at risk, perhaps she could drive to Lake Tahoe this evening and try to conjure it out of the dark. It was a two-hour drive and would mean a late night for her, but she had to try if she could find the right spell.

The pictures of the Aboleth were scary; it looked like part octopus, catfish, and Komodo dragon and seemed to be the size of a whale. She wondered how it had made it out of the suspended-animation prison cell and into the lake without dying. Did it have powers of teleportation, or had someone moved it during the prison escape? If she was Ramsey, she would have placed every awful monster from the prison somewhere on Earth where they could do damage to humans. That would distract the humans from his plan to take over the Earth. She was frustrated by the lack of communication with the Elven Republic. She fixed dinner while studying the grimoire, then sat down to eat and worked out a plan. She thought she should leave a letter behind for Gormon if he returned and for her daughter if the Aboleth defeated her. She wrote quick notes and left them on her kitchen counter. Lake Tahoe was a big lake and she decided to head toward Emerald Bay, as it most likely had the underwater structures that the Aboleth liked.

# Chapter Seven

It was dark when she reached her targeted area that might contain the Aboleth. She had a spell to call forth the creature and a large bottle that she hoped to suck its soul into. The creature wouldn't be dead, but it would be contained until the Elven Republic portaled it away from Earth. She didn't understand how a creature the size of a whale could fit in her jug, but this was magic, and she had to believe that all things were possible.

That said, she was an amateur, a witch of under a week, and she was trying to take on a monster who had injured two strong elves including a well-trained warrior. What was she thinking? Did she want to leave her daughter motherless? She stood frozen on the shore, literally and figuratively as there was snow around her feet. For the twentieth time, she reread the instructions of the recipe to call forth the creature, took a deep breath, and decided to go forward with containing it. She thought of the young man in her emergency room earlier that day and wondered if he would ever be okay. Maybe if the monster was moved to another realm, it would release its hold on the patient's mind if indeed that was what had caused his mental distress that morning.

She put her jug on the hood of her car along with the ingredients for the spell. She had a small lantern, so she read the instructions and could see the ingredients. Occasionally, a car would drive by on the highway beyond her. She hoped that no police would stop to see if she needed assistance. How would she explain herself? They would probably take her into custody for her own safety.

Suddenly, she was startled by the appearance of Gormon. She put her hand to chest, glad he had appeared before she started the spell. "I thought you were injured by the Aboleth? Are you okay?"

"I am healed. I read your note in your kitchen. You are a brave and foolish human."

"No, I'm scared out of my wits, and afraid I'll leave my daughter motherless. I've got this spell to call the Aboleth and I'll stuff its soul into this jar, and you can take it back with you to the Elven Republic. Are you ready? Once I start the spell, I don't want to be interrupted."

"Let me read it."

She frowned at him but shared it. He read it over, looked at her ingredients and her bottle, and said, "This is as good an idea of anything I can think of. Obviously, Michael and I failed in our earlier effort to contain it."

She nodded and began the spell. The only other spell she'd tried was the invisibility spell where she could see Gormon, but other humans could not. This spell was so much more difficult in order of magnitude than that first spell, but at least she had a tiny boost of confidence that the recipe would work.

She laid the ingredients in the correct order and began chanting repetitive words. She moved and mixed the ingredients as instructed. On the third repetition of the spell, she heard a disturbance in the water in front of her. She was dying to look into the water, but the recipe said to hold the bottle in her hand and continue chanting. She moved her attention between the recipe and the bottle as she began the fourth chant and was surprised when Gormon put a stopper into the bottle she was holding.

"I think it is inside. I will drop it off in my realm and be right back," Gormon said as he opened a portal and disappeared.

She started shivering in earnest from the cold and the dissipation of the adrenaline rush. She gathered up the ingredients and the lantern and was about to return to her car. She thought she heard noise in the water, but the creature was supposed to be gone and she didn't have another bottle to contain it. Note to self, bring double the materials the next time she tried to use magic. What if she'd accidentally dropped the glass jug before she got started? What if she wasn't successful and the Aboleth was still out there, and she needed to resume the spell?

She wondered how long she should sit there and wait for Gormon's return. She started the engine to get the heat going and was getting creeped out by what could be out there in the dark. Suddenly he popped into the seat next to her. She put her hand over her chest trying to calm her nerves and her heartbeat. He was quiet, waiting for her to relax, thinking he was observing human meditation.

She opened her eyes and asked, "Did I succeed? Was the Aboleth's soul in the bottle?"

He shook his head, "No. When I reached the castle and uncorked the bottle, nothing but a cloudy mist floated out. I spoke with a warlock, and he said to try it again. He thought you picked the correct spell."

"I don't have another container for it."

Gormon looked around the car and dug up a plastic water

bottle and handed it to her, "This should work."

"It's plastic."

"So?"

"Won't the Aboleth destroy it or bust through it?"

"No. It's not about the strength of the container. The Aboleth is a large creature, but its spirit will be confined to a soul jar. This will keep it from regenerating here. There is no way to kill it."

Stephanie sighed and got out of the car. She had performed the ritual enough times that she had it memorized. She quickly set up the ingredients and went to work chanting the spell. As before, she heard noise from the shoreline. She chanted the spell over and over until she was hoarse in the cold, dry night air. Gormon was watching, standing next to her, and signaled when she could put the lid on. She did so and waited as Gormon opened a portal, and this time he had her step through with him.

Again, she arrived on the castle grounds, but this time there was a group of warriors and what she assumed was a warlock, since he had a different appearance from the warriors. Not knowing what to do, she passed the plastic bottle to the warlock. He grasped her hand to keep it on the bottle and spoke. However, it was in a language she didn't understand, so she looked to Gormon to translate.

"He says that since you captured the soul, you must keep the bottle in your possession. The moment you let go, the Aboleth's soul is released."

"I can't carry around a plastic bottle the rest of my life. If I let it go here, won't it stay in your realm? It can't portal itself back to Earth, right? He's your monster; you folks need to contain him."

The warriors and warlock chatted in what Stephanie presumed was the elven language and, in the end, Gormon directed her outside of the castle grounds to a river. The Aboleth would enter the water and re-create its body, and the elves would deal with it while she returned to Earth. She was exhausted and assumed that Gormon would portal her back to Earth and then, once there, portal the car and the two of them to her driveway. At least she would get to bed soon. Shortly, she arrived at the body of water and after consultation with the warlock she tossed the bottle into the water. She quickly moved away from the water and through a portal. When she returned to her car, she heard nothing from the Lake Tahoe shoreline and assumed she had managed to leave the creature back in the other world.

"Did the Aboleth stay in the Elven Republic?"

"It did, and I am sure my fellow warriors have their hands full," Gormon said with a slight smile.

"Thank you for your help. I can see now I wouldn't have been successful getting rid of that creature without your help."

"No, that was foolish on your part. Let us get into your car and drive slowly. I will portal us to your driveway, so be ready to stop your car quickly."

Stephanie nodded. She was happy the monster was gone, and happy she didn't have to drive home after an exhausting evening. Pretty soon she was stomping on the brake pedal in her driveway. She hit the garage door opener and pulled inside, put the car in park, and turned the engine off. What an unbelievable couple of hours she had just had.

She looked over at Gormon and asked, "Tell me about Michael's and your injuries."

"We tried to portal the Aboleth back to our realm. I admit that I did not read about the creature before we tried that. I thought it was a simple water-based fae, and instead it is much more. I was strong enough to block its mind attack, but Michael was not. He did not move fast enough and got covered by the creature's mucus, which is poisonous. I grabbed Michael and portaled us to the healer's quarters. They are still working on Michael. He will be fine in time, but it takes a while to get all the poison out. I just had mucus where I touched Michael and so I healed quickly."

They walked into her kitchen and Stephanie glanced at the note she had left for her daughter and knew she needed to have a conversation with her—just leaving her a note was so inadequate. She tried to think about where she was in her studies. It was mid-semester, and her daughter was in an apartment about sixty miles away. She would see if they could meet for lunch on the weekend. She needed to introduce her to Gormon as her daughter would mostly think the entire situation was way cool. Stephanie was a widow after her husband died nearly twenty years ago after a freak car accident. She was the only parent her daughter had ever known, and she needed to do better than leaving her a note.

She texted her to see if she had time for lunch on the weekend as she had both days off, as did her daughter. Her response was quick; she had plans for Sunday, but they could meet on Saturday. Stephanie tried to think of a quiet place to have the conversation and introduce Gormon. Finally, she thought of a restaurant that had private alcoves made of velvet drapes. She'd make a reservation there.

"I need to tell my daughter about this mission and introduce you to her on Saturday. Leaving her a written note that I might be dead is a sorry way to communicate with your family."

"It is the principle of the Elven Republic to keep our presence hidden from Earth. Meeting your daughter violates the principle."

"Look, if you hadn't shown up tonight, I might have been devoured by an Aboleth and never heard from again. All my daughter would have had was my lousy note. She lost her father before she was old enough to remember him. I need to try and do better. She's a smart kid and she'll need to see some of the magic to believe me. So, we'll use your invisibility spell. Besides, what if she's a witch as well? I'd like to take the grimoire with me to see if has a connection to her."

Gormon looked pained, but he understood. His own mother checked in on him whenever he was injured. She had tentacles in the royal court and always seemed to know when a healer had to care for him.

Stephanie looked at him and decided that she would have to have him portal into the restaurant and be invisible. Then she decided he might make noise bumping into the table, so he could just arrive with her cloaked in the spell. If her daughter was a future witch, he could sit there the entire time and the two women could speak to him and see his reactions as long as they had a hand on the grimoire, and the public wouldn't see his ears, his swords, or his unusual garb.

"What's your daughter's name?"

"Amelia. Amelia Jones. Hopefully, she'll be a healer one day. On Earth, you attend college to learn book skills for eight years, then you follow behind other healers for another four years. Along the way you specialize in which part of a human you prefer to treat. Some healers deliver babies, others specialize inside the brain, while someone like me knows a little bit of everything as I can handle just about any emergency that arrives."

Gormon looked puzzled at that explanation. Healers were born with the skill in the Elven Republic and there was no specialization. Rather, some healers practiced longer, but as they were long-lived, they all were excellent. Living for centuries gave you lots of time to be good at your chosen occupation, be it healer or warrior.

"Back to the Aboleth—I think he took control of the mind

of a patient who arrived from Lake Tahoe. He was uncontrollable and we had to sedate him. When I read that Aboleths take over your mind, I wondered if this was the source of the patient's problem. I'll know tomorrow when I have a chance to look at his chart. If he is now completely normal because the Aboleth has returned to the Elven Republic, then I'll know what the source of his psychiatric issues was."

"I am sorry you had to contend with that today. We thought it was going to be relatively easy to collect our prisoners with little impact on your world. I think we failed to understand how the population has grown around our prison. Two hundred years ago, there were few if any humans within a day's walk of the prison."

"Yes, our population back then for the entire state was just over a million people. Now it is more than thirty-nine million and Lake Tahoe is a premier and expensive playground."

"Still, I don't think we want to add more fae to this world as we risk discovery. So far, none of your patients have been telling tales of people from my world. Outside of you and soon your daughter, no one on Earth should know of our presence after we collect all the prisoners and depart."

"Let's hope so. I'm going to sleep. Can you review your list again and add some notes about the special skills of the prisoners? That way I'll recognize the injuries that patients may have in my emergency room. Also, here's a question for you—the Aboleth is a water-based creature. How did it get from your prison and into the lake? Do you think Ramsey helped move it there where it would distract from having his plans discovered, or do these creatures sense their natural environment and teleport themselves there? Finally, besides Ramsey, who else can open a portal and disappear from Earth? Think about those questions as you look at the list. Goodnight Gormon," Stephanie said, around an exhausted yawn.

# Chapter Eight

Stephanie awoke after less sleep than she would have preferred, but still she felt a sense of accomplishment that she had helped get that horrible creature off Earth. She also felt a secret sense of satisfaction that she had dumped the monster on the Elven Republic to contend with. She wondered how many healers they'd needed to deal with the creature's mucus before the warlock got him stuffed back into a new jar. He was definitely a really bad fae that she would send immediately to another suspended-animation prison. Everything she read about it indicated that the Aboleth had no redeeming qualities.

Gormon was in her kitchen with a cup of tea when she arrived dressed for work, and ready to eat breakfast.

"At least ten warriors had to be treated for mucus poison before they had the Aboleth contained."

"Hard to believe that we did better than the Elven Republic in containing that creature. We humans are not completely worthless."

"No, you are not. I am learning that you do things differently from us but arrive at sometimes better endings. I do not like these metal boxes you call phones, but they are useful."

"Any word on how Michael is doing?"

"He should be able to rejoin us this evening. As a half-elf, he heals slower than I do, but while he was healing, he had a chance to reconnect with his father and siblings, and King Kanruil commuted his sentence. He is a free man but committed to helping us."

"Excellent! Do you have any answers about how the Aboleth got from the cavern to the lake?"

"Yes, I spoke with the fairy and Michael and they both confirmed that Ramsey teleported the creature to the lake. The Aboleth was not the only water-based creature, however. There is also a Merrow in the lake."

"What's a Merrow?" Stephanie asked, sipping coffee while stirring eggs in a fry pan for herself and Gormon.

"It is about twice your size and looks a little like a mermaid. Except that it has a frightening face and claws that can shred you. They like to hoard treasure, so if there are shipwrecks or are shiny things in the lake, that is likely where the Merrow is located. The good thing about this Merrow is there is only one of them, and he exited the prison without his harpoon."

"Great. I wish we could put out a warning for fishermen to stay out of the lake, but we can't without causing a panic and exposing the Elven Republic. Fortunately, it's very cold now so there aren't a lot of people on the lake at this time of year. I also don't believe the sunset cruise boats and ferries are running. How do we get it out of here? What do you mean it doesn't have its harpoon? Does the same spell work?"

"I do not know about a spell. A Merrow uses its harpoon to drag people into the water where it is much stronger. It can spend time on land, but it is not as effective, and it is relatively unintelligent. I am going to return to the Elven Republic to talk through a few of the monsters on my prisoner list. There are creatures on this list that I have never fought in my three hundred years. Our warlocks can advise us how to deal with some of these and in which order to try and collect the prisoners. My plan of picking off the single prisoners with Ramsey as the final target made sense from a warrior perspective of divide and conquer, but from the perspective of reducing human deaths and injuries, it is the wrong plan."

Stephanie nodded and dished out breakfast to Gormon. He seemed surprised that she cooked for him, but so far, he seemed to enjoy most of what she made, so he shouldn't be surprised that she would put a plate in front of him. She sat down to eat and asked, "While you're conferring with your fellow warriors and elves, could you pop into Earth periodically in case I need your healing? It sounds like there are some scary monsters on your list. I'm worried for my fellow humans."

"Yes, I can do that. There is also a spell in the grimoire that allows you to reach across the abyss from your world to mine."

"Really? Where is it?" Stefanie looked at the grimoire and then at her watch. She was running out of time. She placed their empty plates in the sink. "Show me which one and I'll take a picture of it and study it at work. Do I need any special ingredients for this spell?"

Gormon took a quick look at the spell and replied, "No."

She leaned over the book and took a picture of the spell, then she gathered her stuff and said, "Have a good day."

He nodded and portaled back to the Elven Republic as soon as he heard her garage door open.

Stephanie had an uneventful drive to work and arrived with a few minutes to spare to start her shift. Nothing crazy was going on and the emergency department was relatively empty. Every once in a while, the hospital caught a break, and the staff started the shift at a leisurely pace.

When she had a few moments between patients, she studied the spell. She thought she had it down in case she needed him quickly. Her hospital was the highest-level trauma center in the region, and so they would get any horrible injuries from car accidents, skiing accidents, or now attacks by the fae prisoners.

She heard the base station speaker sound, which meant that the paramedics were trying to talk to the hospital emergency room staff. Sometimes it was routine—they had a chest pain patient on their way in and here were their vitals and an EKG strip. This call was noisy and a bad one. Stephanie could hear the sound of a helicopter in the background.

"Base station, this is California Highway Patrol Helicopter H2o One, we're twenty minutes out with a patient with severe injuries of unknown origin. Patient is a forty-year-old male who called for help from Lake Tahoe after his boat was attacked by a scary mermaid. Those are his words before he lost consciousness. The Coast Guard was able to assist in retrieving his boat to shore and called for our assistance. Patient has deep lacerations and is bleeding profusely. We've started fluids per protocol." The call continued and Stephanie listened and responded with directions. She took a moment and did the spell and texted Gormon. Then she assembled the team that would meet the helicopter on the hospital's roof, including a general surgeon on call. She called the blood bank to send an emergency ice chest of blood units to the department. With any luck they would have the units going into the patient before they hit the elevator to bring him into the emergency department. She hoped she would have Gormon's help, and he could get close enough to the patient to try his healing.

She was about to lead the team to the roof when he appeared next to her thankfully using his invisibility charm. For his benefit and that of the team, she repeated the known facts about their patient, leading the staff, the gurney, and a bed full of supplies to the elevator. Gormon managed to squeeze in, and they headed to the roof. An attendant stayed behind to keep the elevator there ready to bring the patient down to the department.

It was cold as it was still morning, and they could see the helicopter on approach. Everyone kept their heads down and the supplies secured as the big bird landed. Before the blades stopped rotating, the team hustled to begin caring for the patient. The paramedics on board lifted the litter out and onto the gurney. Each person on the team had a role as they moved as one to the elevator. Stephanie was pleased that her prediction was correct, and they had blood flowing into the patient even as they descended into the emergency department.

The patient had lost a lot of blood and had low blood pressure. The paramedics had pumped fluids and applied gauze with special agents in it to stop the bleeding. The patient's worst injury seemed to be in the torso, but there also were deep wounds in his arms. Fortunately, the patient had been intubated in the helicopter, so he was well supported with oxygen. Eventually after a lot of work by the staff, the physicians, and Gormon, he seemed to stabilize. His blood pressure was still low, but he was stable enough to be moved to the operating room for further closuring of all his wounds and then on to the ICU. Gormon followed the patient there. Now the fight for the patient would be blood clots and infection. Stephanie what was in the claws of the Merrow—was there a poison or were they just sharp? Given how cold the lake was, there was not a high probability that there was a lot of infected water in his wounds.

Stephanie sighed and returned to the other patients who had been rolled in while they were caring for the patient. She apologized to them for the wait, explaining they'd had a critical patient arrive by helicopter. Most patients understood, and the one who didn't, Stephanie could tell, was going to be a pain to deal with. Two hours later she looked up and saw Gormon standing at the door to a patient's room. She finished up with the patient and had Gormon follow her to a bathroom.

"How's our patient doing?"

"He is alive, and I think he will survive. I called another healer here and the two of us worked hard, as did your people. The other healer left completely blown away by what he saw healers do on Earth. Your methods are so brutal, but they work. I am not sure we could have saved him if it was just us two healers. All those drugs and fluids and breathing that you do for the patients keep them alive while our healing magic has time to close the patient's wounds and stop the bleeding. Our healers cannot bring someone back from the dead—if the heart stops working, that is it. You do not have to give up, though. It is going to generate some discussion in our realm."

"You're probably exhausted and want to return to your world. Thank you for all you did for this patient. Do you have a way to capture the Merrow, so he doesn't harm any other humans? I heard they stopped boat traffic on the lake while they investigate, but he needs to be gone from this world."

Stephanie heard a knock on the door, and then someone called out, "Dr. Jones, we have a suspected heart attack arriving in two minutes."

She called out, "Be out in a sec."

"We're working on a Merrow solution, and meanwhile we have someone near where he attacked your fisherman, just to keep the humans safe," Gormon said, and then he disappeared.

Stephanie left the bathroom and approached the base station looking for the EKG readout of the incoming patient. After assessing it, she was ready to follow their standard protocol for taking care of a patient like this. The day continued with its usual array of patients. She was glad to see her colleague arrive for the next shift. The patient injured by the Merrow earlier in the shift zapped her strength. Knowing that seconds counted, and good decision making is what kept the patient alive was both exhilarating and exhausting. She took a moment to visit the patient in the ICU to see for herself how he was doing. She approached the unit and introduced herself as she was not well known to this staff. She was pleased to see he was breathing on his own, though he was covered in a swath of bandages.

"He looks remarkably well compared to what I saw this morning. How is his pain?" Stephanie asked the nurse in charge of the fisherman.

"He's improved throughout the day and is healing at a faster pace than anyone has expected, especially given how critical he was on arrival. Even his pain levels are under control. If he looks this good tomorrow, we might be able to transfer him out to the floor unit."

"How about infection? Those gashes were bad when he arrived."

"His temperature and his blood counts are showing no signs so far. So, fingers crossed he escapes that. Besides, as cold as the lake is at this time of year, I can't imagine there was much harmful bacteria in the water."

"Has he spoken about the event?" Stephanie asked.

"A little, and so far that's been the only cause for worry as he's described a monster mermaid as the thing that attacked his boat. We may have to get a psych consult later if he's still hallucinating in a few days."

Stephanie nodded and turned to leave the unit, impressed with how well the fisherman was doing. While some of it was due to her team's competence that morning, she also knew Gormon and his additional healer had had quite an impact on this patient. She felt sorry for him regarding his description of the Merrow. It really was what had attacked him, but no one outside of the Elven Republic would believe him. Soon, she was on her way home, happy to relax with a good meal, a glass of wine, and the grimoire. She really needed to learn the spells in the book. Though she had read the book several times, she tried a different tactic. She looked at the prisoners on the list and then asked herself which spell would suit her best to win in a confrontation. It was a surprisingly relaxing way to spend her evening unwinding from work. Pretty soon, she had a chart going with charms to use on prisoners. Of course, she didn't know what some of the fae species were, and when she tried researching them, they sounded like they were Dungeons and Dragons characters, and who knew if that was correct?

As the night wore on, she began yawning and decided to give up on her chart for now. She had another busy day at the hospital the next day, and maybe she would have additional help from Gormon or even Michael if he finished healing. She looked one more time at the list and wondered which monster she might meet next in person or in her nightmares.

# Chapter Nine

The next two days passed without any surprise patients likely injured by a fae prisoner. She checked in with the fisherman and he was giving up on his story of the scary mermaid, though no one could account for his injuries with any known animals in the Lake Tahoe area. Those investigating his injuries speculated on a bear swimming out to the boat as it was nearing shore.

Gormon had been in and out of her world as he worked on a precise plan for the remaining prisoners including Ramsey. There were still more than forty of them loose on Earth. Today they were driving down the road to Berkeley to meet Stephanie's daughter, Amelia, for lunch. Stephanie carried the grimoire in a bag. She worried that her daughter wouldn't believe her story, and furthermore that she would worry over her mother's mental health. After lunch, they were heading up to Lake Tahoe to try to capture a few of the prisoners on the list.

"It is very important to you that your daughter understand that you are a witch and that magic exists."

"Yes, I realized that when I wasn't sure I would survive the Aboleth. Besides, maybe she's a witch as well. I'm her mother and she needs to know about my new world."

"What if she doesn't believe your story?"

"I expect you to open a portal and take her to the Elven Republic. A few minutes in the castle courtyard should do it. She need not meet your king."

"Do you think it will come to that? She will not believe you?"

"I don't know. Like me, she is very science based and that seems to conflict with magic," Stephanie said.

"We will make her believe."

"If for some reason I shouldn't survive the prisoner round-up, she needs to know why I agreed to participate."

"Why did you agree?" Gormon asked. He thought he knew why, but he was curious to see what she said.

"As a doctor, healer, I took an oath to do everything for my patients including apparently hunting down monsters and prisoners. In addition, there is much to learn about being a witch going forward. Perhaps I can do some good with those powers."

Gormon nodded. He had thought that was her motivation.

Stephanie found a parking space and Gormon walked with her to the restaurant. Stephanie smiled when she saw her daughter was already seated in a secluded booth. Perfect. She paused to give her daughter a hug and to give Gormon time to slide into the booth before her. They dealt with the banalities of the menu and answered the server's question about drinks. Stephanie was nervous and had thought of nothing but this conversation over the past twenty-four hours. She would either lose her daughter's view that her mom was everything she wanted to be as a woman and a doctor, or she would join her on this quest to save this world from a group of fae prisoners. In the gap between when their food orders were taken and when it would be delivered, Stephanie began her story.

"I need to talk to you about something important. This is going to sound like I'm on drugs or hallucinating, but I assure you it's not the case," Stephanie said, pulling the grimoire out of her bag and putting it on her table between them. "Put your hand on this book and tell me if you see anything."

Amelia was puzzled by her mother, but did as she asked, then gasped and jerked back.

"What happened?" Stephanie asked.

"There's a strange-looking man sitting next to you who is only visible when I have my hand on your book," Amelia said, placing her hand and removing it several times just to confirm. Then she left her hand on the book and asked, "Who are you and why are you invisible? You look like an actor from Lord of the Rings."

Stephanie looked around to be sure that their server wasn't about to return. She removed the grimoire and returned it to her bag, then gave Amelia a sheet of paper with the spell that would allow her to see Gormon.

"Here, follow the directions on this piece of paper and tell me if you can see the man after you do everything on the sheet."

It was quiet in the booth as Amelia first read through the directions a few times, then followed them. She smiled after she finished.

"This is the weirdest lunch ever, Mom. Can you make introductions?"

"Sure. Amelia Jones, meet Lord Warrior Gormon Mialynn of the Elven Republic."

"OMG, this is wild. What is going on? Should we order a third meal for Gormon?"

She loved that her daughter's first thought was of Gormon's comfort.

"He doesn't need food like you and I, but we should order a meal to go that he can eat on the way home. He's warming up to human food."

"I think there's a huge story here and I should go home with you to hear all that is going on. I've already done my homework this weekend, and I just have social stuff for the remainder of the weekend that I'm going to cancel. I can take the train back tomorrow evening," Amelia said as her fingers flew over her phone and texting her friends. Then she put the phone down and grinned at Gormon and was about to say something, but their food arrived.

After the server departed, she smiled at Gormon and asked, "Are you an elf?"

"I am."

"Wow. So you can do magic like keeping yourself invisible. You probably don't speak English, but are somehow translating everything we say." Then she thought of something else from her memories of elven stories. "Can you open a portal and move me about Earth? Maybe you could portal me back to school tomorrow night. That would give me more time at home."

Gormon didn't know what to think about Stefanie's daughter. She was the first young human he met. Young humans were much bolder than young elves, who were very respectful of their elders.

Her Mom cut in and said, "Let's finish eating and hit the road, then we can talk without watching our words all the time."

She asked Gormon what he wanted to eat, and she was correct in that he was finding Earth food better than he thought. He asked her to order a salad like hers and she did so after contacting the server. A short time later, they were walking to Stephanie's car.

"Do you need anything from your apartment before we leave?"

Amelia thought about it awhile and shook her head. "I have clothes at home, and I don't need to bring any books with me."

Stephanie nodded and soon had the car on the freeway pointed toward Sacramento. Rather than having her daughter in the back, she had her move up front and Gormon was in the back and still invisible as his clothing and swords would alert other drivers and passengers on the road. She and Gormon began their tale while he munched on the salad.

"Let's start with why Gormon is here on Earth."

"Wait, have you visited his world?" Amelia asked.

"Yes. Accidentally. I'll tell you about that later," Stephanie said, briefly glancing over at her daughter. She was like a five-year-old brimming with excitement on Christmas morning.

"You know, I was worried you wouldn't believe me, but you're a witch too and I'll also explain that to you."

Amelia clapped her hands as if to encourage her mom to get on with the explanations.

"So, there is such a thing as the Elven Republic and it's ruled over by Elven King Kanruil. The Elven Republic has elves, and warlocks, as well as other species such as Merrows, Aboleths, and Redcaps. About two hundred years ago, the Elven Republic built a suspended-animation prison in one of the caverns of a mountain peak near Lake Tahoe. There were no human inhabitants in the area at that time."

"Uh-oh," Amelia uttered.

"Yeah. Last week, the top of the cavern was blown off in an avalanche-prevention accident. There were one hundred prisoners who were released from suspended animation. Gormon was sent by the king to reanimate the prison, but it had been damaged. So, with the help of some of his fellow warriors, he portaled about half of them back to the Elven Republic."

Amelia looked into the back seat and said, "Well done!"

He nodded his head.

"However, that leaves fifty more to recapture. So Gormon started down the mountain following magic signals and sent a few more home. Meanwhile, I had two patients come to the ER at different times in one day. One survived and one didn't. They were otherwise healthy humans enjoying the woods. I couldn't understand what I missed, so when I got home from work, I pulled out a box of books from medical school. The grimoire was at the bottom of the box. I had never seen it before and Gormon says it's from his world. He appeared in my house using his invisibility charm, but I could see him when I had my hand on the book. Imagine my shock at his story, his appearance, and finding out that I can cast the spells in this book; and now apparently so can you."

"This is so cool except apparently some of these prisoners are deadly to humans."

"Exactly our problem. Gormon has healing abilities and has used that skill at work to treat some of my patients. I had a fisherman helicoptered in from Lake Tahoe who was attacked by the Merrow, and I tried to take on the Aboleth by myself. I left you a note in case I didn't survive the encounter. But I decided you deserved much more than that, thus today's lunch."

Stephanie saw her daughter wipe tears from her eyes and she reached over to grasp her hand.

"I survived with Gormon's help, but I need to keep humans alive and help Gormon round up the remainder of the prisoners. There's an evil warlock named Ramsey, who will likely be the last one we capture. He intends to take over Earth. He killed King Kanruil's father before he was sentenced to that prison, and it took many warriors to overcome him and send him to the prison."

"Why doesn't the Elven Republic send more warriors to help? This sounds like overwhelming odds," Amelia asked.

"Earth does not believe in magic, and we need to keep it this way. So, it is just Michael, me, and your mother until we are down to the final battle with Ramsey," Gormon said.

"Who's Michael?"

"It is a long story; just know he's on our side," Stephanie said.

"Okay. I'm on my semester break after Thursday. I'll return home and help. It seems like you need it."

"I want you to stay in Berkeley. This is dangerous work," Stephanie said.

"I'll be back on Thursday. You need my help."

"We'll see," mumbled Stephanie.

Amelia looked over the seat into the back and asked Gormon, "Tell me about you. How old are you? Are you married? Do you have kids? Are you in good standing with your king? What kind of magical things can you do besides healing and portals?"

Stephanie gave another brief glance at her daughter and said, "Is this how you meet new people? You barrage them with questions?"

"Well, I bet you know the answers to these questions already. I'm just trying to catch up."

Gormon replied, "My species as you call it is long lived. I'm just over three hundred years old. We don't marry in the Earth way in my realm, but when we choose a partner, it is for eternity. I have no kids, the king likes me, and I can do various skills with magic like speak to you in English."

He was slightly less haughty than usual as it was impolite to be on your high horse to one as young and enthusiastic as

Amelia. Stephanie supposed a twenty-year-old was just a babe in his world.

"That's rude of me. I didn't notice that you were speaking English and that would not be your native language. I imagine that's a valuable skill if you come from a world that speaks multiple languages—at least I assume that Aboleths, Merrows, Fairies, Redcaps, and warlocks all speak their own species' language."

Stephanie was impressed with her daughter's recall of species names, but she did play the Dungeons and Dragons game on occasion and was used to different species names. In fact, in her daughter's mind, her mother's situation might feel like a game.

"This is true."

"Do you have dragons in your world?"

"No. They inhabit a different cosmic realm."

"I didn't realize there were different cosmic realms. How many are there?" Stephanie asked.

"There are ten. They have different surface geographies and species, and I think one is uninhabitable."

"Have you been to all ten?" Amelia asked.

"No. I certainly would not visit the realm containing dragons unless I had an invite from them."

"Are they huge dragons? Can they shape shift?" Amelia asked.

"I have never seen one in person, but they are rumored to be large; and no, they cannot shape-shift."

"There goes my chance of ever marrying a dragon," Amelia said.

"Seriously? You find out that dragons are real and you're disappointed that you can't marry one?" Stephanie said.

"You have to understand, Mother, that Gormon and everything he says is better than any fantasy story, book, game, or movie I've ever seen. We are riding in a car with a real elf!"

"Yeah, I get that it's cool, but remember you can't tell anyone about Gormon. It's an incredible secret you must keep to yourself. Someday if you have children of your own, you can test their ability to benefit from the grimoire, but you can't tell your future partner or children that you've met a real elf— you'll either end up in a psych ward or be hounded by the paparazzi."

"Yeah, I get it. We'll be witches with a secret and secret heroes for our world saving humans from monsters."

Stephanie pulled into the driveway, and they got out and went inside. It was mid-afternoon, so there was time to round up another prisoner. They needed to study the map and the prisoners.

# Chapter Ten

"How can I help? Is there a charm I need to learn to help?" Amelia asked.

Stephanie hesitated. She didn't want to put her daughter's life in danger, but could she really keep her out of this fight?

"Mom, as you would say, the cat is out of the bag. I'm going to do my best to help you. Yes, I understand it's dangerous, but I'm old enough to make my own decision, and perhaps I can help you return the prisoners to the Elven Republic sooner. Besides, I'll benefit from Gormon's training me to be a witch."

"Let me talk you through what I have seen in the hospital and when I faced the Aboleth." Stephanie spent ten minutes describing in detail what happened to humans who had encountered the prisoners.

"I understand how deadly and painful these creatures are, but we have Gormon and the mysterious Michael to help and heal. Let's not waste time arguing and get on with it. Which prisoners can we locate this weekend and which spells should I practice before we head out? And who is Michael?"

Gormon chose that moment to step between mother and daughter and offer an explanation about Michael. He finished with, "I just checked in with him and he's healed enough to help. He'll meditate until we come upon prisoners and that should complete his healing process."

"Wow, of all the magical things that you can do, I find healing to be best. I accidentally burned my hand in chemistry lab when I splashed acid onto it. Can you heal my burn?" Amelia asked while removing a large adhesive bandage and offering her hand to Gormon.

Stephanie grabbed her daughter's arm to look at the burn with her physician's eye, then passed it to Gormon. Before their eyes, the burn retreated, and the skin healed.

"That is an amazing skill. You could be the most popular person on Earth."

"Yes, but we in the Elven Republic believe Earth is over-populated, so the last thing we need to do is slow the dying process for humans," Gormon said.

"Sadly, that's true," Amelia agreed.

"He is saving humans from the prisoners as they were not expected to die at this time. He also stopped by the children's unit at the hospital and treated all the kids," Stephanie said.

Amelia's eyes watered at the thought that this man who so effortlessly healed her burn, could also stop by a children's unit and save them. She reached over and gave him a hug as he stood there stiffly.

"Okay, let's teach you two spells—one to make you invisible, and the other to see us when we use invisibility spells. It's the strategy to use when you must fight a prisoner," Stephanie said.

"Mom, do you have swords like Gormon?"

"No. There isn't a spell that I've come across that teaches

me sword skills. Just giving me a sword wouldn't do me any good as I don't know how to wield it."

"So, what's our role?" Amelia asked.

"I know the geography. I help Gormon find the prisoners and if there are injured humans, my car and I can treat and transport them, while Gormon sends the prisoner back to the Elven Republic."

Just then Michael materialized in the room. "I've been hearing my name called out. So, I thought I'd show up."

"How are you feeling? What were your injuries?" Stephanie asked, looking him over for proof that he was fully healed. "How did you get here—did you learn how to portal?"

"That monster goo melted my skin off, but with help from the healers, I'm as good as new. And yes, while I was recovering, I learned how to portal as it seems critical to this mission."

Amelia stepped forward and thrust her hand out: "Hi, I'm Amelia, Stephanie's daughter, and apparently also a witch. I'm here to help this weekend and next week after Thursday when college is on a semester break."

He nodded and Stephanie added a few more words of explanation, "On Earth, we go to school for a long time to learn. We start around age five and if you're training to be a healer, you'll finish twenty-one years later, at which time you will enter an apprentice program for another four to six years."

"What a waste of time. When I was young in the Elven Republic, we were tested for our special skills and then sent to train under a senior person," Michael said.

"How do you learn the history of your realm or understand math or learn to write stories in your language or even learn a second language?" Stephanie asked.

"Our parents are expected to tell us the history of our people. We don't learn math beyond addition, subtraction, division, and multiplication, so again, our parents teach us. As for language, unless we are deemed an expert in the language arts, we don't study books," Michael said.

"Wow. That's weird that your species has so little value for education. Do you read fantasy books about humans?" Amelia asked.

"What?" Michael asked, confused as Stephanie and Amelia laughed.

"On Earth, some of us humans spend our spare time reading books. We have books that are non-fiction, which mean they are about real things like travel, health, leadership, business, etc. We have a second category called fiction. These are stories that are not real and are created by the author's imagination. Fiction books have many genres including romance and mystery. We also read a category called, "fantasy" in which there are stories about witches, fae, elves, dragons, etc. We read stories about elves for entertainment. We were merely suggesting your entertainment might be reading stories about humans."

Michael and Gormon had looks of confusion mixed with arrogance as though the elven world would not be entertained by such stories. This made mother and daughter laugh all the harder.

"I needed a good laugh. This is a serious, even deadly situation and laughter reduces the stress and anxiety of the moment," Stephanie said.

"Is that what they teach you in your apprentice programs?" Gormon asked.

"It is actually proven science on Earth. You may want to have your healers reach out to me so I can show them the evidence to make their healing more effective."

They just shook their heads. All joking aside, they went back to studying the list of prisoners and the map.

"We have two fae prisoners called Korrigans. The sisters

were sentenced for murdering menfolk as that is what they do. They come out only at dusk or night, and they're about the size of a child though they look like adults. Michael and I are sensitive to their wiles. You women are not. They can move at lightning speed and change shape. They can kill with their breath. We have a charm we can use to block their breath from reaching us. Let's look through the grimoire to find a similar one for you witches," Gormon said. "I should be able to sense their location in the woods. I will also have to warn the warriors at the other end of the portal to likewise use a breath-prevention charm."

They practiced the charm to make sure everyone could be safe around the Korrigans and not breathe their air. Then they piled into Stephanie's car and headed out toward Lake Tahoe. Gormon could sense the different species' magic signals and directed their path. Soon they zeroed in on the Korrigans' location and found a parking spot. They headed into the woods, invisible except to each other and able to avoid the breath of the Korrigans. It was dusk when they came upon the two women. They were the size of children and despite the cold, they were dressed in white gowns with their signature red hair. They were speaking in a language that Stephanie and Amelia couldn't understand.

Stephanie stepped on a twig, and it snapped. The two Korrigans stopped their conversation, said something, then sprinted out of the area. Gormon took off after them and Michael followed. The Korrigans and the elves moved at superhuman speeds. Stephanie and Amelia soon lost the four fae to the woods.

"What should we do now?" Amelia asked.

"First. maintain the invisibility spell. We don't want the Korrigans or frankly a black bear to see us."

"Can bears smell us?"

"I don't know. Either we'll find out when one chases us or perhaps Gormon might know the answer."

"Should we stay where we are so we don't get lost and so the guys can find us?"

"Gormon seems to be able to find us by our magic signals. I recorded the geo coordinates of where I parked the car, so we should be able to find our way back."

Amelia nodded and said, "Then let's follow their path to the degree that we can and see what we find. We need to ask Gormon if there's a magic tracking spell in the grimoire."

"Actually, I made a copy of the book in case I need to use it at work, and it's on my phone. Let me do a search for 'magic sensing' and see if I can find a spell for us."

Stephanie's search was slow as cell towers were sparse in the Sierra Mountains given the terrain. She watched for a while and wondered why it was so slow as she downloaded the grimoire. If it was on her phone, why did the towers matter? Sigh. Finally, she had an answer to her question—it appeared that there was a spell to source magic. She read the description and realized it was less sophisticated than Gormon's ability. He could sense each magic species; all she could do was sense whether there was magic. The only way she knew she was sensing magic was the purple halo that had appeared around Amelia. She then had Amelia practice the grimoire's spell and she saw the purple halo around her mother.

"Life is never going to be the same after this," Amelia said.

"I know. I've been thinking about spending my next vacation in the Elven Republic to see if I could learn any of their healing arts. I realize we are an overpopulated planet, but if I could at least save the children and young mothers that come in with trauma, then I want to try."

"Oh, Mom," Amelia said, giving her a tight hug. "This is so complicated. These elves have amazing healing skills, but when we humans use them, it somehow feels that we are making judgements on which human life is more valuable."

"I know. If you and I are the only two humans on Earth with these skills then we cannot heal all the sick people. Frankly, it's a little like that now. Who lives after traumatic injury often depends on how close the nearest trauma center is located. The other skill I would love to learn from the Elven Realm is pain relief. If I could put my hands on someone in horrible pain and take that away, that would be awesome.

"We probably need to put aside these medical ethics questions and concentrate on the problem at hand. Let's walk in the direction we saw Gormon disappear to and look for purple haze. By the way, you still have your Korrigan breath avoidance spell in place, right?"

Both of them repeated the spell just to be sure, and they began walking in the direction they had last seen their elven friends. There were very faint swirls of purple guiding them that must have been left behind by the four magical creatures ahead of them. They picked up speed with Stephanie watching the swirls and Amelia using a flashlight as dusk was closing into night.

"I wonder if there's a limit to the number of spells we can use at the same time. We have the invisibility spell, the magic detector, and the don't-breathe-Korrigan-breath spell. I wish I knew another witch to ask that question," Stefanie said.

They both quieted as they heard voices up ahead in a language they didn't understand. Amelia turned the flashlight off as they were close and there was still enough light to see.

When they arrived in a bit of a clearing, Gormon was coughing and about to pass out and they helped him down to the ground, getting the swords on his back out of the way. Stephanie guessed immediately that the Korrigans had got him somehow. She went into doctor mode and said, "Gormon, I'm going to breathe for you. Michael, either figure out how to portal us to the Elven Republic or go get your best healers and fetch them here. Amelia, we're going to do mouth to mouth. We'll alternate every 30 breaths." Everyone nodded and Stephanie began blowing air into Gormon's lungs once his chest was no longer rising and falling.

Michael disappeared from sight and Amelia asked, "When it's my turn to breathe, answer this question. Do elves breathe at the same rate as we do?" She was counting aloud so they would know when to switch.

Stephanie took a couple of breaths of her own and said, "I don't know. Judging by Gormon's inability to use his limbs, I suspect that the Korrigans' breath contained a paralytic rather than something allergic that would have seized up his airway." They were almost at the switch again when Michael material- ized with someone. "Amelia, you keep breathing while I talk to the healer."

However, there was no need as the healer knelt and placed her arm on his chest. Amelia and Stephanie were about to switch again when they felt Gormon stir. He looked blankly at the people standing around him before his brain engaged. The healer said something to him, and he nodded. Then he seemed to communicate back to her telepathically. She nodded.

"My name is Nienna Glavien and I am a healer. I see you breathed for Lord Gormon when he could not. I have not seen that before, but it saved his life. I would like to learn from you."

Gormon whispered with amusement, "I am just glad you did not have to cut me open to save me."

Stephanie found herself blushing from the praise and Gormon's mild amusement.

"We teach something called cardio-pulmonary resuscita- tion, or CPR, for humans. It's a way to sometimes save the life of someone who can't breathe or whose heart stops. It doubles and triples their survival rate until more sophisticated help can arrive. I'd be happy to teach your healers the technique. With humans we breathe fifteen times a minute, but your variety of races may require something else." Stephanie's mind was already off thinking of a lecture she would design with the variable of fae species, oxygen, and ambu bags. She also made a note to herself to add an ambu kit to the backpack she carried on these prisoner-hunting missions.

"How did you know I would not poison you?" Gormon whispered, but his voice was getting stronger.

"I didn't, but you said the Korrigans kill men with their breath, so between being female, a human, and the spell, I'd hoped that it wouldn't affect me. If it did, I hoped your healer would arrive in time to save us too."

"You and your daughter are very brave. Thank you for saving Lord Gormon," Nienna said.

"You're welcome, but I'll admit, it's also the faith I had in your healers. I've watched Gormon, who is not a healer, counteract the poison from other fae, so I imagined that a healer could do even more."

Gormon gained enough muscle control that he could sit up, and the healer moved her hand to his shoulder, sending more healing energy. Stephanie reached for his swords and handed them to Michael to put back in their sheaths. She didn't know anything about swords and feared she would put them in a position to slice Gormon's back if she got it wrong.

"Michael, what happened with the Korrigans? How did they see you? I didn't have time to hear the story before this emergency started. Are they still close by?" Stephanie asked.

"The Korrigans can move fast and shape-shift. Gormon and I took off after them, but we didn't bother with our invisibility charms as they knew we were looking for them and we no longer had the element of surprise. Then we came to this clearing with Gormon in the lead. One of them had shape-shifted into a horrific flying creature and flew right at Gormon. They made this sound with a large exhale and then flapped their wings to send at his face. It was mere seconds, but I think it was an extra-large breath that blew at Gormon, and we were panting slightly from our run. Would you agree, Gormon?"

He was about to answer when Nienna replied, "Your protection spell likely was not up to the task of protecting you against a large dose. I think your Korrigans have experience using that deadly skill and knew what to do."

"Yes, they were sentenced to prison for the murder of other fae," Gormon said.

"Gormon, it's getting late and while you're regaining your full strength, I think it would be wise to end the search for the Korrigans now. I have some equipment—specifically, special masks that will protect you and Michael from the Korrigans. I think it is better to head home, sleep or meditate in your case, and come up again in daylight. I realize that the Korrigans are usually only sighted at dusk or night, but they're somewhere in the area and your magic species detector should be able to find them. Nienna, I would love to train your people, but let's make it after we finish collecting all the prisoners. Does that sound like a plan?"

Gormon was able to rise with the additional healing touch from Nienna. She made sure he was stable then stepped back and said, "I will speak for Lord Gormon. He should meditate now to finish his healing and I like your plan, Stephanie Jones. I will open a portal and see that all of you get to Stephanie's home. We will see each other soon."

"My mode of transportation is nearby, so I need to go there. Why don't you portal us there and Gormon can meditate on the ride home? As a healer from this world, I'd like to keep an eye on him to make sure he doesn't relapse."

"He will not relapse, but I understand your concern."

Soon they were back at the car and the healer was gone. Gormon sat beside Stephanie so she could keep an eye on him while driving. Soon he was in a meditative state despite the motion of the car on some of the curves of the road. Michael was likewise meditating. Amelia was writing something down, and when she finished, she grabbed Stephanie's phone to study more of the grimoire.

# Chapter Eleven

Once they reached home, Michael and Gormon went to one of Stephanie's guest bedrooms to meditate. She asked them if they wanted food, but they shook their heads. Meditation was more important. She entered her kitchen and began to prepare a meal for herself and Amelia, who pitched in to help in a well-practiced routine.

"I made a list of supplies for a first aid kit that I believe you need to carry based on what I saw today. Of course, you know this better than me, but it sounds like the prisoners are getting deadlier. What were you going to do if Michael hadn't found a healer?"

"I was going to leave you alone performing mouth to mouth and have Michael portal me to the supply room at the hospital. In less than three minutes I think I could have returned with an ambu bag and oxygen. If after, say, thirty minutes of bagging, Gormon didn't respond, I think I would have found an adult transport ambulance and borrowed a ventilator that is battery operated."

Amelia smiled and said, "I knew you would have a backup

plan. Do you think any human drugs would have reversed the paralysis?"

"I don't know but add that to your list if it's not already there. I'll want some bandages that slow down the bleeding, an EpiPen to undo any allergic reactions, some pain killers, and something we can use as a litter. Gormon is a tall person, and I don't know how we would have moved him from the clearing. I also hope Michael improves his portal skills so he can be of greater help."

"Can I just say it's cool that you might be training elven healers? I'm CPR certified, so perhaps I can come along and be your assistant. I'm dying to visit another world. This has been the most exceptional day of my life. We are so lucky to be who we are and where we are."

Stephanie smiled at her daughter's enthusiasm and said, "I wonder how they'll react to an ambu bag and mask? They'll need different shape masks for the different fae. It sounds like the fairy that Gormon found near Lake Tahoe was smaller than most birds. They probably have craftsmen that can design the masks for the fae. Then there is the heartbeat. How many different heartbeats do they have among their species? Does everyone even have lungs and hearts? I'm not going to worry about that. I just feel privileged to share what I know and perhaps learn something from them. What if I could do a better job at healing or pain relief here if I learn a technique from them? Nienna reversed the paralytic poison in Gormon. What if I could learn to do that for overdoses in the hospital? First, though, we need to focus on capturing these prisoners."

"Are we going after the Korrigans again tomorrow?"

"I assume so. I'm going to get a special re-breather and stock my backpack before we head out again. I can get a special mask at a home improvement store, and I'll stop by a pharmacy to pick up a few drugs and bandages. Maybe when I'm at work on

Monday, if I have time, I'll look at what supplies are in the tool kits of paramedics. I actually should carry an emergency kit with me regardless of the fae."

"I think for the first time in my life, I don't want to return to school. I'd rather stay with you until you round up all the prisoners. I want to help and I want to learn about the Elven Republic and my magic capabilities. Is there a spell to help me do well on my final exams?" Amelia said with a smile.

"My daughter will not cheat on her exams! I'll examine the grimoire for that spell and if it's there, I'll rip it out of the book, so you're not tempted. This prisoner round-up quest may look like fun, but as you saw, it's dangerous work. When we get toward the end of this round-up and go after Ramsey, Gormon says the Elven Republic will send us many warriors as that is what it will take to defeat him. Imagine how dangerous that is going to be."

"Come on, Mom, I have straight A's. What if I could move that to perfection and get 100 percent on all my exams rather than 95 percent?"

"Your professors would know that you're cheating and so would I," Stephanie said as she moved their plates to the kitchen table to sit down and eat.

"Yeah, you're right about cheating. Our plan for tomorrow is to go out and get a few supplies, then we'll head back to the mountains and see how many prisoners we can capture. If the Korrigans come out only at dusk and night, where do you think they'll be?"

"I wonder if it makes sense to talk to an anthropologist in the Elven Republic to understand the skills and habits of these prisoner species. Maybe I'll ask Gormon if such an expert is available, and he can bring them here or we can go there. I know he has some of this knowledge in his head, but I doubt he knows all the customs of all the species—he probably only knows how they fight and kill."

"I'd love to visit the Elven Republic for any reason. You were going to tell me how you ended up there."

"We were driving on Interstate 80 to recapture Michael, and Gormon mentioned that he thought he should have amnesty and not return to prison. He was sentenced for wanting to kill the current king's father, who was a bully about mixed species like Michael. Ramsey actually killed that king, but Michael spent two hundred years in prison just for his thoughts. If he was willing not to try to kill the current king, then he would get amnesty. We wanted to have an offer before we cornered Michael. So Gormon opened a portal for himself, but I guess because we were in motion, my car and I joined him going through the portal. We landed on the grounds of the royal palace with me slamming the brakes on the car. Fortunately, traveling through a portal slowed the car down; otherwise, I might have hit the palace walls at seventy miles an hour."

"That's a story to tell for all time. Did the fae scatter when you came to a halt?"

"They did, and they wondered at the contraption we call a car. We had a quick conversation with the king and then returned to the car; and this time, I drove slowly, and we exited the palace walls and rolled into a deserted parking lot in the forest near Michael."

"What an adventure! I'm so grateful you decided to come and talk with me. If one of these prisoners succeeded in killing you, I would wonder the rest of my life what happened. Now I feel a duty to join you in this battle and I'll learn a lot along the way about our world, their world, and my witch capabilities."

"Let's change the conversation to something else and forget the fae for a while. How do you like your apartment and your classes? Are you still thinking of following in my footsteps and going to medical school?"

"Yes, now more than ever. If I can learn something from the Elven Republic that makes me an even better doctor, that would be cool. We need to study the grimoire and understand how we can use it at the bedside. I bet there's something in there for pain control."

"So, we're back to the Elven Republic discussion. That was a quick detour. Here's the thing about the grimoire—I don't know why it ended up in my box of books from medical school, especially because it's a book from Gormon's world. I don't know any other witches to ask questions of—for example, it seems that most of the spells are self-spells, like we can make ourselves invisible. The only outward spell so far has been the one that allows me to see Gormon and Michael through their invisibility spells."

"We have much to learn about this grimoire and the spells we can cast. Do you think there's a spell for cleaning your laundry or vacuuming your house?" Amelia asked.

"Somehow, I doubt it. I also wonder if the book is its own sentinel being and it adds and removes spells as people need them. I ponder that question because I feel like I discover something new every time I crack the book open."

"How about if you compare what you have on your phone to what's in the book?"

"I think I'll leave that question to be answered later. I'm tired, so let's hit the sack, and I'll leave a note for Gormon about the sociologists or anthropologists among his elven folk. Maybe he'll have an answer in the morning. Regardless, it's back to Tahoe."

"We could have Gormon portal us there instead of driving."

"Yes, but if anyone is wounded and we need to get out of

there, the car is the best choice. Besides, I like the supplies we can put inside it."

Amelia nodded and they walked off to their respective bedrooms.

The next morning when Stephanie walked into her kitchen, Gormon and Michael were already seated there with her note between them.

"Good morning! How are both of you feeling this morning? Are you fully recovered?"

"Of course we are. Meditation always heals and strengthens elves," Gormon said.

"I'm sure you have species experts in your realm; I just don't know what they are called. Do you understand what I am looking for?"

"We were just talking about who might have detailed knowledge of our species and we alighted upon our Moon Elves."

"What's special about them that would help us learn about the fae prisoners on your list?"

"They are known for traveling far and wide and have great tolerance for other species. Their travels may gain us some routine knowledge about the species on the list."

"Can we go talk to them about our list before we set out? I'd especially like to know what the Korrigans do in the daytime."

Gormon thought about where in his life he'd come across Moon Elves as they weren't usually found on the palace grounds. He had been on missions for the king that took him around the realm. He had met them somewhere. Then he remembered. He had journeyed to Cloudholde located on the far eastern border of the realm. It was far away from the king's palace and a likely place for most Moon Elves to travel to. He decided he would try to portal there to see if he could find someone with the knowledge that Stephanie was looking for.

"There is a city on the far side of the Elven Republic where I recall coming across some Moon Elves. They are always out exploring the realm. I am going to portal there with Michael and we will see if we can find someone knowledgeable as I do not disagree with what you are asking about these prisoners."

"Okay, but don't be gone too long as we need to head up into the mountains," Stephanie said.

"I think you should leave ahead of us, and I will find you when I return. If you leave your car where you did yesterday, I will try to bring one of the Moon Elves with me for a conversation."

"That sounds like a good idea. I need to pick up some supplies here before I head up, so we'll be there in about three Earth hours. Even though your phone doesn't work in your realm, it will keep time for you as I know the concept of Earth hours is different from time in your world."

Gormon nodded and he and Michael disappeared. She wondered if they ate and then remembered it wasn't high on their list of important things to do. She'd cook breakfast for herself, and leave a plate for Amelia, and then set off to buy the supplies.

Then she got a text from one of her colleagues. There had been a disaster and a ski bus had overturned with sixty people on board. The most severely injured were being airlifted and bused to her hospital; other injuries were being distributed to other nearby hospitals including in Tahoe. If she was in the area, they needed her at work for the mass casualty event. She replied that she would be there as soon as she could. She texted Gormon about the change in plans, and she performed the spell to send him the message across the realms, then texted her daughter. She knew she could have woken her up, but she needed to leave as soon as possible, so texting was faster.

She was driving to work thinking about the bus. A crash in

March, when the skies were blue and there was not a winter storm, was unusual. Now, with every strange event in the Tahoe area, she was going to wonder if the prisoners were somehow involved. Soon she arrived at the hospital and went to work dealing with broken bones, back injuries, concussions, and lacerations needing closure in a young healthy population. They were fortunate that there were no minors on the bus as that would have added another layer of complication. The bus driver was a few decades older and had injuries, but as he was wearing a seatbelt when the bus rolled, his injuries weren't as severe as they could have been. Sadly, there were a few deaths at the scene. A few hours later, the chaos was under control, and she knew she could leave the remaining patients to her colleagues. It was midday, and she still had the Korrigans on her mind. She texted Amelia that she was on her way home, and then checked in with Gormon to see if he was in this realm. He texted back that he was. So, she called him.

She realized that she hadn't trained him how to answer a call, and as an elf he wasn't necessarily attuned to what red and green buttons signified on Earth. So she texted him again telling him to hit the green button when she called again.

This time the call connected, but he didn't speak. So she said, "Hello and hold the phone up to your ear," hoping he would get the hang of it.

Finally, she heard a "hello" back. "I'm on my way home. I'll be there in about twenty minutes. Did you find a Moon Elf who was knowledgeable about the various fae species?"

"Yes."

"Okay. I can tell you're very uncomfortable with this phone. We'll talk when I get home."

She was tired from the post-adrenaline rush of the mass casualty event. She didn't want to waste energy on a call going right. Once they were in the car, Amelia could teach Gormon and Michael how to answer calls. She also didn't have the energy to beef up her first aid kit. Perhaps Amelia had gone shopping in her absence for the items that didn't require a prescription. With the Korrigans, the most important thing was likely the masks from the home improvement center.

She walked into the house to find a new representative of the Elven Republic looking around her house with wonder as Amelia explained how things were used on Earth.

"Hi everyone. Sorry, I got called in to work to help with a bus crash that caused many injuries. I'm Stephanie and I'm what you would call a healer in your world." She put her hand across her chest as she had seen the elves do.

"Mom, this is Cellica Umexina. She's a Moon Elf from the city of Madspire. Did I pronounce those names correctly?"

The Moon Elf nodded.

"Welcome to Earth. As I'm sure Gormon explained, we're trying to round up fae prisoners that are on the loose on Earth and harming humans. In this world, we have sociologists and anthropologists who study cultures and can tell us about their behavior. I understand a Moon Elf is the closest thing that the Elven Republic has to that concept as you interact with a lot of species in your realm. We need to find two Korrigans. What do they do during the daytime? Are they sleeping, meditating, or what?"

"Yes, Lord Mialynn asked about that and explained my role in helping you understand the various species," Cellica said in a soothing voice. "I'd ask what a bus crash is, but it sounds like you have more important things you wish to discuss."

Amelia took a moment to pull up an image of a bus and explained it to Cellica.

Stephanie wondered if her voice was as beautiful in every language she spoke.

"Korrigans are out and about in daytime, but you likely

don't recognize them. Their hair is dull, their eyes red rimmed, and their skin is very wrinkled. They avoid being seen as they know they don't look as pleasing in daylight as they do at night."

"So how do we find them?" Stephanie asked.

"Same way you did before. Didn't Lord Mialynn use his magical senses to find them? He can do so again, and they'll likely be as hard to capture. They will move fast and change shape."

"Did you come across any Korrigans that were nice in your travels?" Stephanie asked.

"Yes. Not all the Korrigans have been sentenced to prison for murdering menfolk."

"What makes them evil, then?"

"I do not know. They are friendlier to women. I do not know how to set up a portal, and from what Lord Mialynn said, you ladies also are unable to open portals. I would say leave the men here and we'll capture them, but then we're stuck as we can't get them back home to the Elven Republic. Lord Mialynn, can you stand inside a circle where the outer rim represents a portal, and you just need them to attack you from any angle and they'll enter the portal?"

"I've never tried that. We can do that now. Let's go into the back yard and we'll try it."

The five of them walked into Stephanie's backyard. The three women stood close to the house. Gormon stood in the middle of Stephanie's grassy backyard and then tried creating a portal in a circle around him. He tried at least five times, but as he moved in a circle the portal moved with him, never forming a complete circle.

"Is there a brilliant warlock at home you can ask for help?" Stephanie asked.

Gormon looked disgruntled at her suggestion that a warrior needed help from a warlock, and said, "No."

"How about if instead of doing a circle, you do an umbrella-shaped portal?" Amelia suggested.

"Umbrella?" Gormon looked puzzled.

"Just a minute," Amelia said, running inside the house.

In no time, she was back and demonstrated an umbrella.

Gormon tried that shape and on the third try succeeded. He had Michael try the umbrella-shaped portal and he disappeared, only to return shortly. He then tried the umbrella portal on Gormon's backside and again it worked as they hoped.

"Okay, we are good to go. Cellica, would you mind coming with us and maybe my daughter can take notes about what you know about the species of prisoners on this list?"

"I would love to travel and see more of Earth. Amelia and I will chat."

Stephanie nodded and they went out to her garage and entered her car. She had the gas masks from the home improvement store, but she doubted that she could convince her two men to wear them for their own protection.

She took the same route as yesterday to find the Korrigans, while listening to Amelia and Cellica chat about the various species' behavior and the things they were seeing on the road. Like Gormon and Michael before her, she was fascinated with what humans had done with technology, yet there was a lack of magical skills. They arrived at the parking area they had been in the previous day, which was also where Gormon still sensed the magic signature of the Korrigans.

After exiting the car, Stephanie asked Cellica, "Were you able to complete your comments about all the prisoner species?"

"Yes. There were a few on your list that I have not seen on

my journeys through our world, but I also don't know another fae traveler that might have interacted with them."

"I'll open a portal so you may return to our realm," Gormon said.

"Thank you, Lord Mialynn. This has been a most interesting adventure."

Soon Cellica Umexina disappeared back to wherever Gormon had found her.

"Are elves or fae formal in their language? I noticed she always called you Lord Mialynn," Amelia asked.

"We are formal people. Also, it is a sign of respect. I am called Lord Warrior Gormon Mialynn as I have accomplished certain tasks. I am a warrior as I have participated in my share of battles and lead my people. I am a lord because my king anointed me as a reflection of my duty and accomplishments for him."

"We have lords, ladies, princes, sheiks, dukes, kings, queens, and other titles, but they are inherited titles. In America, we have no hereditary titles, because our founders wanted elected leaders," Amelia said.

Gormon didn't reply to that, but merely nodded.

Amelia asked Michael, "Can you achieve those titles some day?"

"Possibly. Lord Warrior Mialynn has a two-hundred-year head start on me. I wasted two centuries in suspended-animation."

Amelia put her hand on his shoulder, "But now you have a new lease on life and a bright future. On Earth, people are wrongfully sent to prison on occasion, then they get released twenty or thirty years later when new evidence is found. On Earth we age, so our prisoners may go into prison in their twenties, but then get released decades later when times have changed. It's awful."

"Only an Earthling would have such an odd comparison. Two hundred years and I don't age, or thirty years and I come out a middle-aged man, with the shorter time served a worse deal."

"Yes, and I suppose we'd better concentrate on the problem at hand. Gormon, you've notified your realm that we're sending them Korrigans. So, we'll just walk into the woods and stand back while Gormon tries to attract two older, red-eyed, wrinkled women to visit him under his portal umbrella," Stephanie said.

He nodded and Stephanie held her hand out as if to say, "You first."

They walked on a trail roughly toward where they met the two women yesterday with Gormon in the lead and Michael following him. Stephanie and Amelia held back a distance behind Gormon as she didn't want to accidentally touch his portal and she wanted to give him the opportunity to attract the women into the portal. She saw two somethings approach him fast and then they disappeared into thin air. She hoped that was the Korrigans disappearing into the Elven Republic.

They stood still until Gormon turned around and said, "They have returned to the Elven Republic."

Amelia couldn't help herself. She clapped her hands and said, "Well done."

# Chapter Twelve

Stephanie sighed and looked over the list, and said, "We have time, who should we go after next on the list? Do you sense any fae beings around us?"

"Of course I do. There is a dwarf closest to us, so let us talk about him first. He was sentenced as he made magical weapons for Ramsey to use to try and take over the kingdom. I am surprised that he is by himself rather than with Ramsey. He has the power to enchant things. He was not sent to prison with any weapons, but he may have made some by now."

"It is interesting that he's by himself. Does he have a family back in your world?" Amelia asked. "Cellica said that most dwarfs are very social beings."

"Should we make contact with his family in the Elven Republic to get his backstory, or do you have it in your head?" Stephanie asked, pointing to her mind. She hoped to find more stories like Michael and the fairy that Gormon met at a nearby cabin—fae creatures that were unjustly sent to prison.

"Let's return to your car, and you three can wait there while I contact his family. It should not take more than an hour, and I think you will have to move your car to be closer to the dwarf."

They nodded and did as he suggested, while he portaled back to the realm.

"Did you reconnect with your family while you were recovering from the battle with the Merrow?" Stephanie asked Michael.

"I did, and I'll admit it was awkward. The healers brought my father to the House of Healing. My mother died a long time ago."

"Did your father remarry?"

"No. Elves marry forever. Often after one spouse dies, the other soon follows as they have lost a part of their soul. In the case of marrying a human, an elf knows they will spend centuries without a spouse, but they can't remarry as we are a monogamous species, and you violate that principle even if it's the afterlife. Our gods would frown upon it."

"How did your father find a human to marry? I thought you avoided interacting with Earth?"

"When the original elves came to Earth searching for a place to build their prison, my father met my mother. She was a witch like you, and your world doesn't have a great record at dealing fairly with witches. She knew she would be safer in the Elven Republic, but she didn't expect the king's attitude toward her and her children. She wouldn't be killed in the Elven Republic, but her children—my sister and I, would be made miserable."

Stephanie nodded, thinking of the Salem witch trials which would have been at least a century before Michael's father visited Earth. "Did your sister visit?"

"No, mostly because there wasn't time. After I redeem myself here, we'll meet."

"Was your father disappointed in you for being sentenced to prison?" Amelia asked.

"Yes and no. He understood that I was bullied, but elves are less emotional than humans and he couldn't understand why I had thoughts of killing King Bully. He also understood that I was unlikely to carry out my thoughts, and he thought being sentenced to forever in suspended-animation was unduly harsh. He's happy to have me back and likes that I'm being mentored by Lord Warrior Mialynn as he has a good reputation in our realm, and he believes that I'll be returned to him when we're done here."

"I think your previous king was horrible and your sentence ridiculous. We humans are very emotional, and I have to think that many of us have wished someone dead. We would have run out of room in prison if we were sentenced for our thoughts," Stephanie said.

"Tell me about how dwarfs enchant things. Why are they able to do that?" Amelia asked. She often lost at her local Dungeons and Dragons game and wondered if a small side benefit of helping round up the prisoners might be better game performance if she knew more about the species one encountered in the game.

"Good question. They don't cast spells; rather they use runes and craft them into objects."

"What do they need to craft objects? Are they blacksmiths or carpenters, or something?"

Michael looked confused at her question and responded, "They primarily work with stone. I'm not sure what a blacksmith or carpenter does."

Gormon reappeared outside of the car, and he opened the door and took his seat to talk to them.

"The dwarf's name is Skar. He made weapons for Ramsey because this evil warlock held his wife hostage. His wife is still alive but in ill health as dwarfs do not live as long as elves. He has one child alive as well. He should be easy to convince to return to the Elven Republic. Like Michael, if he agrees not to join forces again with Ramsey and fight to overturn the king, he will be pardoned. Furthermore, the king would like him to make weapons for our warriors to use to fight Ramsey."

"What a sad story. After we get his affirmative response that he won't try to overthrow the king, can you portal him to his wife, and can he make weapons there? He sure sounds like he has a motive to work with us," Stephanie said.

"Yes. That is my assessment as well."

"As a human, can I use a magical weapon?" Amelia asked.

"Yes, if you are instructed in its use," Gormon replied.

"Cool."

"It's not cool. It's not cool that there are prisoners on the loose here on Earth injuring humans. It's not cool the four of us must risk our lives to capture these species," Stephanie said. "It's not cool that Gormon would have died because of the prisoners if you and I hadn't done mouth to mouth. Sorry about ranting, my dear, but you have the enthusiasm of youth for a video game, but this is real life, and we could do more than die on a video screen. We might end up totally dead."

"You're right, Mom, sorry. I haven't come across the term *totally dead*. Is that more dead than partially dead?"

Stephanie sighed, smiled, and hugged her daughter, "You know I'm a mama bear when it comes to your safety. I need you to take every precaution so we both can come out alive at the end of this adventure. Okay?"

Amelia nodded, then Michael asked her, "What's a video game and what's a mama bear?"

"I'll show you in the car. Perhaps we'd better head in where Gormon directs us."

Stephanie moved the car a few miles away, parked, and

again they went into the forest using their invisibility spells. They came upon a small clearing in the forest where a short man with a long beard, odd clothing for Earth, as well as boots sat contemplating his world. He looked sort of sad, although it was the first time Stephanie had seen a dwarf in person, so who was she to judge his emotions?

Gormon took the lead and asked in another language, "Skar?"

The man looked up, then squinted as Gormon undid his invisibility spell. It was Stephanie's sense that the dwarf felt slightly comforted by the clothing Gormon was wearing. The other three dismissed their spells as well.

"Yes, who goes there?"

"I'm Lord Warrior Gormon Mialynn of the Elven Republic and King Kanruil's representative. I have an offer for you from the king, but I am going to spell you so you can understand the four of us as we speak the human tongue."

"King Kanruil? Is his father dead?"

Stephanie and Amelia looked at each other thinking the current king's father was turning out to be an extreme jerk.

"Yes, he was murdered by Ramsey shortly after you were sent to prison, which was just over two hundred years ago," Gormon said.

"Two hundred years?" There were tears running down his face and into his beard.

Stephanie put her hand on the dwarf's shoulder and said, "Sir, your wife and son are still alive. We would like you to be reunited with them, but we need to understand what is going on in your head."

Skar just had more tears run down his face, then he whispered, "I only made those weapons for Ramsey because he kidnapped my wife. I'll always choose her over the king, any king."

"Yes, King Kanruil realized that you made a tough choice. If the king keeps your wife safe, do you promise to support him? We have a battle with Ramsey coming up and we would like your help with weapons," Gormon said.

"If the king will keep my wife safe, I will help. However, can't Ramsey portal home at any time and kidnap her again?"

"The king, and more particularly the warriors, can keep you and your wife safe. We cannot stop Ramsey from portaling back to the Elven Republic, but we do have an alert should he try. We have heard from other prisoners that he intends to take over Earth as he knows there are no magical beings here."

"Yes, when we first came out of suspended-animation, I was one of the first people he teleported out of the cavern as he said I was critical to taking over Earth. I looked around at the dozens of other prisoners he needed to manage, and I ran away as far as I could go. I don't like the cold, but I didn't know how to get home. Thank you, Lord Mialynn, for sending me home. I will make weapons to help you defeat that evil Ramsey."

With a few more questions to be assured of his loyalty, Gormon and Skar were on their way back to the Elven Republic and Skar's wife. Stephanie thought it must be hard on the dwarf as he didn't age while in the suspended-animation prison, but his wife had. She would look old, and their marriage was denied two hundred years of bliss. Oh well. At least he had a son. Then she thought of a new question.

"Michael, what is special about dwarven weapons?"

"Dwarfs use runes to add power to weapons. So they can be faster, stronger, sharper, or whatever someone needs."

"How were they used by Ramsey in the last epic battle?" Stephanie asked.

"I don't know as I went to prison just before that."

"I'm sorry you lost so much time when your crime wasn't that bad," Amelia said.

Stephanie was starting to worry that her daughter might be attracted to Michael. The elves were a beautiful race and even though he was only half-elf, he was a good-looking man. He was also centuries older than her daughter. She wondered how they would craft a life between Earth and the fae realm. Then she lightly slapped her cheek as it was bad to plan her daughter's life at this moment in time. She was just being an overzealous mother.

"What should we do now? I would think Gormon would be tied up in the Elven Republic for at least a few hours. I think we should return home and wait for him there, unless, Michael, you have the ability to sense the other fae on our list and there's one close by? Of course, if we do capture him, you would need to portal him back to the Elven Republic. Are you able to do that?"

"I'm not sure. Let me try to portal you with me."

"What happens if you don't have the portal ability to bring a second person with you? Do I end up halfway between Earth and the Elven Republic?" Stephanie asked.

"No, you just end up never moving and stay here. I know because I tried it when I was home."

"Ok. Let's try"

After a few minutes, they knew Michael could portal another species with him to the Elven Republic from Earth.

"We don't want to take on a dangerous species without Gormon here. Can you identify any prisoners nearby that are on our list and likely won't kill us?" Stephanie asked.

Michael studied the list and thought about his brief interaction with other prisoners while they were still in the cavern.

"There's another elf on the list who's also a half-breed like me—half dwarf and half elf. He murdered someone representing the king in self-defense. So, he has the ability to be more violent than me, but he was taunted for a lifetime, just as I was, by the king and his minions. Let's approach him with our invisibility spells, and I'll try and have a conversation with him."

"Ok. How far away is he? Should I move the car?" Stephanie asked.

Michael paused, trying to hone his senses for detecting magical beings. Gormon had centuries of experience more than he did. After concentrating, he said to Stephanie, "I don't know distances on your Earth, so I don't know what to tell you about moving the car."

"Can you stay invisible and portal to where the prisoner is and turn on your phone using the coordinates?" Amelia said.

"I don't understand much of what you just said. Can you show me?"

Amelia gave him an overview of geo coordinates and then opened his phone to the Compass function and showed him how to record it. Soon he was off and then he returned. Amelia and Stephanie were able to look at the map and determine that they needed to move the car.

A short time later, the three of them were walking through the woods, invisible to all around them. Stephanie needed to remember to ask Gormon if the invisibility spell also hid their scent. This forest contained a lot of big bears, and it would be helpful to know if their scent as well as their person was invisible to the bears.

They reached the space where the prisoner was located, and Michael spoke to him in the fae language. The man responded and a conversation briefly occurred. Stephanie and Amelia could only stand there waiting for Michael to say it was safe to turn off their invisibility spells and relay what the prisoner had said to Michael. Stephanie wished she had asked his name, but she forgot. The man stood up and aggressively approached them.

Stephanie wished she understood what had been said and if Michael was in danger. Then Gormon appeared beside her and took in the situation at a glance.

"Stop!" Gormon commanded in a thunderous voice. Even if the dude didn't understand the word, he would have understood the intent of the word. So he stopped a few steps from Michael. Gormon then said something more and the conversation reverted to English.

"What's your name?"

"Wallamir."

"I am Lord Warrior Gormon Mialynn and King Kanruil's representative. Yes, his father is dead and has been since shortly after you were sent to prison. I am going to portal you back to the Elven Republic and you can discuss your situation with the king's representatives. Two hundred years have passed since your entry in suspended animation, so things may appear different to you." With that, Gormon opened a portal and dragged Wallamir through and they were gone.

"Let's return home now. I think our work is done for the day and you can tell us what he said once we get to the car," Stephanie suggested. Amelia and Michael nodded.

Once Stephanie pulled onto the road, she asked Amelia, "Can you look through the grimoire to see if there is a translation spell? I don't want to be cut out of conversations again. Besides, it would be helpful for my patients if I could use a spell to hear and speak their language."

"That's a brilliant idea, Mom."

"Michael, what did Wallamir say?"

"He recognized me from the cavern and knew I had been a fellow prisoner. He asked if I was joining Ramsey's group and I said no. Then he asked what I was doing, and I said helping round up the prisoners to return them to the Elven Republic. Before I could explain that times were different, he started to charge me and then Gormon appeared. I don't know what they will do with his sentence. He was bullied like me, but while elves are generally peace-loving folks, dwarfs have a bit more of a temper. He reacted by using his superior strength and he ended up killing an elf. The realm will have to decide what to do with him. I certainly think he's served enough time, but he needs to control his temper, perhaps the healers can help him with that."

Stephanie nodded. It wasn't her problem, but she was glad the Elven Republic would look for ways to help Wallamir and perhaps he could be safely released. They continued on their way home and found Gormon waiting for them in her kitchen.

# Chapter Thirteen

"Hello, we're done for the day. We resolved four prisoners on the list. Amelia needs to return to her apartment, and I need to find a translation spell. How did it go with Wallamir and the court?" Stephanie said upon sighting Gormon.

"Wallamir will remain in custody for a while. Our healers will evaluate whether he has the potential to kill other people and assess how he will behave among our people. They realize his anger came during a different time. Also, he has served two hundred years already. Is that enough? It is out of my hands, though I did tell folks he did not harm you three and came willingly.

"I was so busy fighting on behalf of the kingdom against Ramsey, I do not think I realized how awful life was for half-breeds or even how much the king's father made it worse. We hear about the chaos here on Earth and we think the Elven Republic is a more reasonable and just world, but then I look at what was done to Michael and Skar and wonder who needs to be sent to prison indefinitely other than Ramsey," Gormon said with a sigh.

"Are there other prisoners on the list that are mixed-species as we would call them here on Earth?" Stephanie asked.

Gormon shrugged and looked at the list again. "I think there might be as many as five."

"Does the Elven Republic have any other off-world prisons with similarly unfair sentences?" Amelia asked.

"I do not know. I will ask someone in the court the next time I visit."

"I need to return to my apartment at college. Gormon, can you portal me there?" Amelia asked.

"How about your roommate? Will she see you appear out of thin air?" Stephanie asked.

Amelia looked at her watch and said, "She should be at work at the moment. However, just in case she took the day off, you can portal me underneath a large oak tree near my apartment. Even if someone was walking by, they would think I just moved around the trunk of the tree."

Gormon waited for her mother to agree and once she nodded, he moved closer to Amelia, who raised her hand in a stop gesture, ran quickly to her mother to hug her, and then moved back to stand next to the elf. He opened a portal, and they were gone. He arrived back a few minutes later.

"Did she arrive safely?" Stephanie asked.

"Of course," Gormon said with a stiff upper lip.

Stephanie had to turn away while she smiled. She didn't think the lord/elf/warrior man would appreciate being laughed at for that stiff upper lip. She decided to change the subject.

"I realized today that I need a translation spell so I can understand what your various species are saying. Frankly, it would also be useful at work as many people in this region speak many languages. I looked through the grimoire, but I didn't see a translation spell. What suggestion do you have that would help Amelia and me?"

"Are you sure the book doesn't have a translation spell? Often, when you place the book on your lap and think about a spell that would be useful, the grimoire produces such a spell."

"Oh, I wondered if the book did something weird like that; even though I copied it to my phone, it seemed like it had different spells when I looked at it later. I'll try for a translation spell now."

She did as he suggested and sure enough, the grimoire produced a translation spell. She tried and then looked up at the two men and said, "Say something in your language."

They did so and she understood. She searched for a Spanish station on her television and again she could understand the speakers. Then she wondered if she could speak back to the person in the language she was hearing.

"Can you speak again? I want to know if I reply to you, will it be in English or your language?"

They again experimented with language, and she could swear she was speaking English, but it was sounding like another language. This was so weird and so exciting. She wondered what the long-term impact of learning spells and being a witch was going to be like. If she learned nothing more than this translation spell, then it was an incredible lifelong gift that excited her more than any other spell. For the rest of her physician life, she would be able to communicate with any patient speaking any language. Wow.

That reminded her she would be back at work the next day. "Guys, I have to return to work tomorrow. I'll find out more about that bus crash as it seems suspicious. I think you should try to meet and return the mixed races and anyone else on the list for a minor crime. Just curious, but do you have any other suspended-animation prisons?"

"No. It was a project of the former king. There are many things we do not like about that prison. Now, we do not send people to prison for two centuries. The current king did not know about this prison until someone in the prison guard ranks brought it to his attention after the cavern was blown off and the cell re-animated. It has been my experience so far that about half of the prisoners we have returned have been immediately released, while others have been evaluated and released."

"What will they do with some of the more violent species like the Aboleth or the Korrigans?"

"The Aboleth will be moved away from any population centers to another side of the realm where there is another Aboleth. They will either kill each other or have companionship. It will be away from other fae species that they can harm. The healers will have another go at trying to heal the Korrigans' minds and if that fails, they'll go to a new prison." Gormon said.

"Why didn't the king's father try that two hundred years ago?"

"Because one of the reasons Ramsey was so powerful was that he figured out how to use species like Aboleth to his advantage. He managed to place the Aboleth in the waters closest to the palace. It was one more deadly thing we had to fight."

"How did the current king have no knowledge of this prison on Earth if Ramsey killed his father? Wasn't he in charge at the time?" Stephanie asked.

"The Elven Kingdom was in chaos. The new king had much to organize and learn, and yet grieve his father's death. At that time, we managed to capture Ramsey and give him over to the guards to control; they knew of the suspended-animation prison and sent him there. It was never a decision of the current king, but based on everything that Ramsey has done here on Earth, I think it was a wise decision for the Elven Republic."

"Perhaps for your world, but not our Earth. We've had

humans die and be badly injured because of that prison. I wish the prison guard leader had said something earlier to the king, and perhaps you could've moved the prison back to your realm and evaluated the sentences of some of the prisoners like Michael and Skar."

"Yes, we have a saying in our realm of, 'take care of today, so tomorrow is better'; we did not do it in this case."

"Yeah, we have a saying like that on Earth: the future starts today, not tomorrow. I'm going to cook dinner now and I'll make a meal for you guys. Cooking relaxes me. It's my form of meditation. I can pull up another episode of Star Trek for you if you like."

"Yes. I like that show," Michael said, while Gormon frowned. Stephanie was amused that a full elf was dour in personality, while a half-elf had a more emotional personality. Score one for the humans.

Stephanie set up the show for Michael and was amused when Gormon sat down on the sofa after removing his swords to also watch the episode. Tonight, she was going to make chicken, piccata, a salad, broccoli, and quinoa. It was all-natural food and shouldn't upset the digestive systems of elves, yet it would feed them extra protein for the battles ahead.

As they were eating dinner, Stephanie said, "I know I showed you how some things work on Earth, but if you want to shower or wash your clothes, I can show you how to do that."

They both looked at her blankly, then she sniffed them and studied their clothing. There were no stains or tears. She could detect no body odor, greasy hair, or dirt on their bodies. Perhaps they had a magic system for keeping them and their clothes clean. No time like the present to ask.

"On Earth, we use soap and water to wash our bodies, our clothing, our cars, our pets, and nearly every surface in our houses. We have bacteria everywhere in this world. They can cause disease. Bacteria can also cause body odors that make people stink. How do you stay clean, and how does your world stay clean in the Elven Republic?"

"We have what I believe you call bathtubs, which we enjoy on occasion. We have spells or brownies to keep our clothing clean and in good repair. We have waterfalls in the Elven Republic which sound like your showers," Gormon said.

Stephanie was puzzled by the term, *brownies*. And asked, "What are brownies? On Earth, they are sweet treats that we bake out of chocolate and eat. Somehow, I think you have a different definition of brownies."

"Yes. Brownies are a type of fae that like to keep households clean. They are tiny creatures and they do an excellent job. However, if you're not kind and polite to them, they will leave."

"As they should. Your waterfalls sound like our showers. In fact, some of our shower heads are called 'waterfall.' However, our water is heated. I would think your waterfalls are cold, or do you have a spell to heat the water before it hits your body?"

"The fae can cast a spell before they step into a waterfall that will heat it up to a certain temperature. As for soap, we have many plant leaves that serve that purpose."

Stephanie nodded and offered a glass of wine to her guests. She smiled as they each took a sip and frowned, then took a further sip and set the glass down. She would be the first to admit that wine was an acquired taste. She wondered about the palates of elves. Did they like sweet or sour? Did they like salt or other savory flavors? Just more to add to her long list of items to learn about the Elven Republic.

While they ate, she had another thought. Her laundry had been piling up as she tried to manage three jobs—learn to be a witch, assist the fae representatives with collecting prisoners, and working full time as a physician in the trauma center of the region's largest hospital—and she hadn't had time to do laundry. Was there a spell in her grimoire, or could the men sitting across from her do it for her? After they finished the meal and she cleared the dishes, she returned to the grimoire to look for a useful laundry spell. She placed it on her lap, put her hand on it, and three times in a row nothing happened. No spell was offered by the book. She looked up to Gormon who was smiling.

"What's so funny?"

"You were picturing a laundry spell so loudly that I could pick up your brain waves for the first time. A grimoire is not to be used to avoid activities you can do, but don't want to. While you sleep tonight, Michael and I will take care of your laundry."

Stephanie thought of the two men she was on a quest with handling her bra and panties and decided, no thanks. She would buy new clothing before resorting to elf laundry.

"That's okay. I have plenty of clothes to see me through another week. You gentlemen go ahead and practice your meditation, and I might see you before I head to work in the morning. Good night."

They nodded as she left the room.

"Are you going to get her clothes clean?" Michael asked Gormon in the elven language after she'd left.

"Of course. I can cast a spell that will clean her clothes and fold them, and I'll leave them on that table as I don't know where or how she puts them away," Gormon said, pointing to a large dining room table. "They'll be cleaned without us touching them. She certainly has done a lot for us including saving my life."

They watched a few more episodes of this Star Trek show. It was strange how humans entertained themselves with fiction stories. They liked the character of Spock as he reminded them of their species, but while his personality matched theirs, his appearance did not. They judged their host asleep, so Gormon began pulling clothing from her bedroom. He soon realized there were two types of clothing. That which was hanging on something and that which arrived without the object. He sensed these were clean clothes and changed his charm to request clothing that was not hanging on the object. This time he saw a few items of clothing with blood on them. Healers from his world never got body fluids on their clothing, he thought in disgust. Still, his charm cleaned all the clothes and nicely folded the items in an organized pile on her large table. He and Michael headed to a room that was comfortable to rest and meditate.

They were still meditating or asleep when she awoke the next morning. She went out to her kitchen to grab a quick breakfast before heading to work. She wanted to see if there was any more information on the bus accident. She saw her clothes neatly piled on the dining table and stopped, then walked over to the piles. She picked up something that she knew had blood on it, but it was gone. There were no body odors coming from any of her clothing. She didn't know how he did it, but she would assume there was some spell that didn't require that he touch her clothes. She just couldn't see Gormon with the stiff upper lip folding her clothes in neat little piles. She smiled as she exited her garage for the journey to work.

She arrived at the hospital and between patients tried to find out more about the bus crash, but apparently, she was the only person who was curious about it. Likely only the bus driver would know what caused him to lose control of the bus, and he was at another hospital. A government agency would investigate the crash given the injuries and fatalities and maybe she would find out more then. She was pleased to get through the day with no patients arriving who were likely injured by one of the prisoners.

Stephanie was about to leave when she got a text that both guys were injured. Michael was the less injured and would be coming via portal to pick her up and take her back to Gormon. She asked for a few minutes as she needed her coat and her medical bag. She had Michael meet her at the car.

She had no idea how the two elves could pinpoint locations they had never visited before, but they did an awesome job finding her. She arrived at her car with her supplies at hand and texted Michael that she was ready. About three minutes had passed. He appeared and he had a bad gash on his upper arm. She stepped closer and they were off to wherever Gormon was located.

Stephanie always had this weird feeling when she exited a portal. She had this suspicion that she should count her fingers and toes to make sure they all made it along with her body. It was dark now, but there was a light lit near Gormon. He was lying on the ground with his eyes shut.

"What were you fighting?" Stephanie asked as she knelt down next to Gormon. She took his pulse, but decided she should ask the two of them what their normal pulse was later. Michael sat down exhausted from trying to heal his wounds yet needing to fetch Stephanie. It was then that he asked himself why he hadn't gone to the Elven Republic for a healer, and instead had fetched the Earth doctor hoping she wouldn't cut Gormon open like he had mentioned.

"We don't know. We sensed additional half-species in this area and were following a path toward the magic source. Out of nowhere something hit Gormon in the head and sliced my arm. It's gone now, but Gormon hasn't recovered consciousness, and my wound is surprisingly not healing."

"Do you know where Gormon was struck? Do you know what caused your wound? Was it a sword?"

"I don't know. I didn't see anything."

Stephanie knelt at Gormon's side and checked him over. She could find no wounds. He was breathing. She started running her hand over his head searching for a lump. Gormon seemed in no immediate danger other than he wasn't conscious.

She turned her attention to Michael. She washed his wound with something she had in her kit. She then applied a bandage that promoted coagulation so the bleeding would stop. She also gave Michael a sip of a protein milkshake. He didn't like the taste, but he could feel his energy returning.

"I could sew up your arm, or if you feel up to returning to the Elven Republic, you could bring Nienna back."

"No offense, Stephanie, but the thought of you sewing up my skin as though I was a purse is a scary thought. Your drink helped a lot. I think I can make it back to the Elven Republic and spend time searching for a healer to come back with me."

Michael stood up and Stephanie turned her attention back to Gormon.

# Chapter Fourteen

Stephanie ran her hands over Gormon's body looking for injuries but found none. She especially felt around his scalp for a lump, but she came up empty handed. It was cold and creepy in these woods, and she worried about whatever attacked the two men could come back. She tested his lower limbs for sensory movement and saw that his reflexes were intact. So, no spinal cord injury that she could sense without the diagnostic tools of a modern hospital. He was lying on his swords, so she moved him minimally to get them off his back. He would be more comfortable, and she would have a weapon she didn't know how to wield, but it was better than twigs or trying to slug someone with her stethoscope.

She pulled an aluminum emergency warming blanket out of her backpack and covered him with it, which also gave her something to kneel on without her soaking her pants in the snow. Without help from the Elven Republic, she would have called 911 for help, but it was worth waiting for Nienna to arrive. She thought about taking his blood pressure, but she didn't know what a normal reading was for his species. She might suspect a diabetic coma, but this was a battle injury, not a medical condition; and with magic in play with these prisoners, the diagnosis could be completely new to her. Note to self, see if you can visit Nienna after work tomorrow to learn more about treating her two warriors.

Stephanie looked at her watch, wondering what was taking Michael so long to return. Maybe when you were weak you traveled more slowly through a portal? However, they seemed to move fast from the parking garage to here. Maybe Nienna took a while to find, but he had found her quickly last time. Maybe she was treating Michael's injuries before they returned. All Stephanie could do was keep watch and make sure that Gormon remained breathing and take her mind off what might be in the woods. If your average bear that regularly roamed these woods approached, her sword wasn't going to do much good. Another note to self, get a veterinary tranquilizing gun to be used if a bear or a fae approached when she was alone in the woods.

Finally, she sensed movement nearby and looked over hoping it was friends rather than foes. To her horror, it was a black bear. She had no food on her, though the empty protein milkshake container was nearby. She grabbed the sword and made herself big, as that was supposed to scare bears away. She also remembered she was supposed to make noise, so she started hitting her stethoscope against Gormon's sword to make noise. Finally, the bear turned away and ambled off. Whew. Then she thought she heard another sound and looked down to see a puzzled expression on Gormon's face. He was awake!

She quickly knelt next to him and asked, "What is your name?"

She was assessing him for a concussion or even brain damage.

"I am Lord Warrior Gormon Mialynn. Why are you asking

me such a dumb question? What is this thing on me and why were you banging the metal thing against my sword."

Okay, no concussion with all those questions.

"Michael and you were injured by something he didn't see. He was able to portal me from the hospital parking lot to care for you, and once he had his strength back enough to portal between worlds and retrieve a healer, I sent him to the Elven Republic to find Nienna, but they haven't returned, and it's been at least fifteen minutes. As to why I asked the question of 'who are you,' I was checking for a concussion, which is a brain injury in humans. Can you move your legs?"

He demonstrated by moving his legs up to ninety degrees and the blanket fell off him.

"What is this for?"

"It's a warming blanket. You were lying in the snow unconscious, and I was trying to keep you warm. I removed your swords from your back to make you more comfortable and so that I would have a weapon until help arrived. I was banging my stethoscope head against your sword to scare a large bear away that potentially wanted to eat us."

"Why didn't you create a protection spell around us?"

"Because my brain was focused on what conditions would make you unconscious, and I was frustrated over my lack of understanding about elven vital signs and healing."

Gormon sat up and thought about standing up, but somehow knew he was not up to doing that yet. He did take a moment to set up a protection spell around the two of them. It seemed he had more to worry about in these woods than just fae prisoners.

"What are these vital signs you mention?" His brain was slowly engaging its gears.

"Can you tell me first what happened in case you lapse into unconsciousness again?"

"We were attacked by some projectiles. I had my shields up, but whatever it was hit the shields so hard that it squeezed my brain. I had a terrible headache and then I dropped to the ground in pain. That is the problem with shields. Whatever the projectiles were must have scratched Michael. I don't understand why he hasn't returned with Nienna. I wonder if there was poison on those projectiles?"

He started to get up slowly, and Stephanie gave him a hand for balance. He looked like he merely tolerated her assistance. To give him time to right his world, she told him about human vital signs and her desire to spend some time one evening with Nienna learning about the various fae vital signs.

He stood up straight and immediately reached for his swords, which seemed to be a bad idea. Stephanie noticed the same bear approaching so she grabbed one of the swords to make the same noise. This time the bear didn't back away and it continued forward until it met the shield around the two of them. It body-slammed the shield a few times, and let out a roar.

Stephanie looked around for her supplies and spotted them, hopefully within Gormon's protective spell. She saw him pick up his sword, and she put a hand on him to stop him.

"First off, the bear is really strong and you're still recovering even though you think you're Superman. I'm tired of being Lois Lane to your Superman. Second, the bear lives in this forest and we shouldn't kill him or her in their house. Third, what if it's a she and she has cubs nearby? You don't want to make them orphans."

He looked down at her with his normal haughty expression and asked, "Who is Superman and who is Lois Lane?" He put his sword down and they watched as the bear hit the shield a few more times with both his head and his claws. Stephanie remembered she also had a protein bar in her backpack.

"Can I throw something through the shield?"

"No. Why?"

"I just remembered I have a protein bar in my pack that is likely attracting him. I'd love to throw it to him."

"We could time it to put the shields down and fire the chocolate bar at the bear."

"You're starting to sound like Spock on Star Trek. I'm ready when you are. Do a countdown of 3-2-1 when the bear isn't surging toward us, and I'll pitch him the food."

They watched and he counted down and she threw the bar. The lousy protein bar wasn't even big enough to be an appetizer for the five-hundred-pound bear, but hopefully he would move away now that the scent of food was gone. Beside them Michael and Nienna appeared, and they quickly threw up their own shield when they saw the bear.

"Are you too weak to kill it?" Michael asked Gormon.

"No, I am not! She would not let me kill the bear. It wants food, and she gave it one of those nasty tasting protein bars."

"That will be a deterrent; the bear won't come back to her for any food if that's all she has to offer," Michael said.

"Considering that a bear regularly rips apart humans stupid enough to sleep near food, and then eats them, intestines and all, I don't think we can say that a bear has a delicate palate."

They watched the bear sniff the air some more and then it wandered off into the woods. They regrouped into a circle with a larger shield around them in case any other intruders arrived.

"Lord Mialynn, Michael said you were knocked out by something. I am glad to see you on your feet, but allow me to heal you some more," Nienna said. They waited in silence as she put her hands over Gormon's ears. After a time, she stepped back and said, "That should do it. Does your head feel better?"

"Yes. Someone threw projectiles at my shield so hard that

they hurt my head. Whatever the projectile was, it skimmed off my shield and tore into Michael's skin. Was there poison in it? Stephanie mentioned that Michael was slow to heal."

"Yes, Lord Mialynn there was poison, but it is gone now and Michael has healed. That's what took us so long to get back to you. The poison's damage was boosted when Michael portaled back to the Elven Republic. So we had a lot of work to do to heal him. A dark elf or warlock must have created that special poison knowing that you would return home to seek care."

"Yes, that feels like something Ramsey would direct."

"Nienna, before the men were injured, I was thinking I would like to spend a few hours in the Elven Republic learning more about your species. On Earth, we monitor something called vital signs. This is a patient's temperature, heartbeat, respirations, blood pressure, and sometimes oxygen saturation. I would have loved to evaluate Gormon that way, but I don't know what your normal values are," Stephanie said.

"It sounds like you should come teach our group of healers as we don't do any of those measurements to judge whether someone is healthy or not. Instead, when we place our hands on the body, we can tell what's wrong and send healing energy their way. We can tell if something needs healing, but we don't measure the degree of healing needed. We would also like to learn your skill of mouth breathing for our people."

"So what's the difference between what you can heal and what Gormon can heal? He has healed an entire hospital unit of sick children. I can teach you mouth breathing, but I would like to bring my daughter and some equipment as it is easier to demonstrate with two people. Perhaps we can also talk about which species of the Elven Republic you heal. You have some outright monsters in your realm that I presume you wouldn't attempt to heal. Equipment and knowledge about mouth breathing would depend on species."

"My healing abilities have greater speed and depth than the average elf. All elves and some other species have the ability to self-heal. Even humans don't die with the first injury. However, elves are essentially immortal, and when we get tired of living, we can will ourselves to death. We can also be killed in battle. Lord Mialynn has less power to heal than I do. So in the case of Michael and poison, you want me to be the healer rather than Lord Mialynn as poison is harder to reverse. The longer poison is in the system, the more damage it does and the more effort it takes to reverse," Nienna said.

They made plans to meet up in the evening after Stephanie left work the next day. Gormon would take care of portaling her to Nienna's healing space. She would discuss CPR with the elven healers, but she wouldn't teach it until they had some data on normal vital signs for their various species. Gormon opened a portal for Nienna to return to their realm.

"So, what do you think attacked you?" Stephanie asked.

"We were looking for a different type of elf, called a Wood Elf. He was sent to prison for injuring members of the king's army. He did not kill anyone, so we thought he would be reasonable to talk to. We were wrong," Gormon said.

"How about what Nienna said—the projectile was poisoned specifically to make it worse for you to portal to the realm? Is that something this Wood Elf could do, or is that your dark elf at work?"

"I still believe the wood elf would not have the ability to do this on their own. I am not sure how I would put an agent on a projectile that accelerates the spread of poison when someone goes through a portal. I am trained in all manner of warfare. Most Wood Elves are poorly educated as they live in the woods and are solitary. Understanding Michael's and my behavior would not come easy to this elf. This was a sophisticated attack."

"How did he attack the king's army before?" Michael asked.

"I do not know, but I will find out."

"Well. I'm a tired human. I put in a long day at work, and now I've been in the cold woods for an hour or so. You can portal us home or to my work parking structure so I can get my car. If we go home, I'll need one of you to get me to work in the morning."

"I will take us to your home and one of us will take you to your work tomorrow," Gormon said.

Moments later, Stephanie was removing her coat inside her kitchen. It was good to be warm again. Since she was tired and didn't feel like cooking, she ordered enough Chinese food from a local restaurant to feed the three of them. Then she looked over at her dining room table.

"How did you clean my clothes? I noticed the blood stains are gone," Stephanie asked, as she gathered the first pile.

"Apparently the magic that cleans and repairs elven clothes works on human clothes. Once you were asleep, I started pulling clothing from your bedroom. Some of it came out hanging on a metal device. I concluded that those items were clean as care was taken with them. So, I recast my spell to exclude the metal item. Would you like the piles moved to your bed, so you don't have to carry them?" Gormon asked.

Stephanie looked at him with an expression somewhere between amusement and amazement, but nodded that this would be helpful. By the time the doorbell rang with the food delivery, all her clothing was put away. She vowed to find a laundry spell. Her warrior's spell had done a better job with stain removal than she could. She liked the idea of saving water as California was always short on water.

She brought the food to the dining table and explained what it was and how to use chopsticks. As throughout her medical career she often had to eat fast, Stephanie also set out forks for the food. She didn't bother with the chopsticks but was amused with the men trying to get the hang of it after she demonstrated their use. They both succeeded in picking up their food but soon went back to the forks.

"I love this wide selection of food on Earth. I think it is the one thing I'll miss when I return permanently to our world," Michael said.

"You could always portal back here and get take-out food. You will want to dress more like an Earthling if you do that, but you could arrive with hot food very quickly. Or you could pick a cuisine or type of food that you like, study how it's prepared, and open a restaurant in your world," Stephanie suggested.

"That's an interesting idea. I don't know what I'll be doing after this mission is over other than getting reacquainted with my family."

"You could become a warrior and learn fighting skills," Gormon suggested.

"After being away from my family for two centuries, the last thing I want to do is take a job that will send me away from them across the realm. So, no thanks."

"Do you have food establishments in your realm?"

"Yes. Though not as many or with such variety as you have here. We have game we can kill to feed us on missions."

"There are many parts of the Elven Republic that seem intriguing, but food is not one of them. Unless Michael opens a food establishment, I won't be asking to be portaled to your world to eat."

"Maybe instead of opening a restaurant, I should just open a delivery service where I fetch food from Earth's restaurants," Michael said.

Gormon frowned at this idea while Stephanie clapped at the great idea.

"We have many delivery services here that use cars or bicycles, and your portal service would be faster at getting the food delivered. The only problem is that you can't call in the order and have it waiting for you when you arrive. You would also have to match your service hours to Earth's hours, though with your portal ability you could find great food at any time somewhere on Earth."

"I'll investigate this idea once we have rounded up our prisoners. Maybe Nienna, Gormon, and Cellica could be my test cases, then I'll go from there."

"How will you pay for food on Earth?" Gormon asked.

It was as if he stomped on the brakes to the food delivery dream joyride that Michael and Stephanie were having. They both looked shocked that they hadn't figured out this key question.

"Do you have nickel, gold, silver, or cobalt available in the Elven Republic?" Stephanie asked.

Michael looked to Gormon for the answer.

"Yes."

"Bring it to Earth and sell it for your starter cash. Have your clients pay you in natural resources that you can then sell on Earth," Stephanie suggested.

"My father likely knows about these natural resources. I'll talk with him."

"Not to change the subject, but how many prisoners did you reclaim and return to the Elven Republic today, and how many are left on your list?" Stephanie asked.

"We found six and returned them to the realm, so we are down to fewer than forty. Other than Ramsey, we've returned some of the most dangerous to humans on our list."

"Yeah, I can't imagine the damage a giant could have done

to humans and their cars and structures," Michael said. "I remember a giant from when I was growing up and it was huge."

"Is anyone on your list likely to be pardoned by the king?"

"Pardoned?" Gormon asked.

"It's a term where a high official in the United States—a state governor or the president— can have someone released from their sentence. Their criminal act is 'pardoned.'"

"I guess we have something like that. The king and a few other people have that right. Yes to your question; about half were immediately pardoned, and the other half are awaiting evaluation. If we find them working with Ramsey, that changes the king's representatives' willingness to pardon their prison sentence."

Stephanie nodded and asked, "Have you asked Skar to start making weapons yet?"

"No. I need to sit down with my fellow warriors and discuss what we need. Perhaps I'll do that while you sleep tonight," Gormon said.

"I'd volunteer to come with you, but I don't know what I can add. I'd rather talk with my father about natural resources, as Stephanie called them. This food is really good, and I'd love to import it to the Elven Republic."

"We didn't finish it all. Why don't I send you home with a heated container so your father can try this food? I'm afraid that without trying some of the food on Earth, he may not see the value of your future business," Stephanie said, getting up from the table to do just that.

Soon both men were gone on their respective tasks, and the house was quiet. It had been a wild week so far, and tomorrow would be another day at work doing a job she loved followed by a visit to the Elven Republic to learn from their healers.

# Chapter Fifteen

Stephanie was cooking breakfast for herself when Gormon appeared. She was glad he had remembered she needed a ride to work since she'd left her car there the previous evening. If he hadn't shown up, she would have called a ride share service, but with his ability to portal her anywhere, she didn't lose time commuting. Instead, they both cast invisibility spells, then portaled to her car. They looked around and waited for someone walking nearby to pass by. Stephanie ended her spell and returned some items to her car that she had removed the night before. Then she waved to Gormon and walked into work.

She was excited to arrive at work and excited to be able to exchange information that evening with the elven healers. Then the day began to go downhill. After several days of routine patients, someone from the Elven Republic was out shooting humans with the little arrows again. She took a minute to cast the spell to communicate with Gormon if he was off-planet as well as text him. She was pleased to get a return text that he could meet her at her location. She met him in the bathroom and briefed him on what was going on. They had three patients who were crashing from a blood pressure perspective.

"I don't think you can focus on completely healing one patient at a time as the other one or two might die. Can you give a quick healing boost to each and then concentrate on ridding them of the poison?"

"I'll do better than that. I'll get Nienna here to help."

"Awesome. Keep her invisible too."

He nodded and they went to work. Stephanie approached the sickest patient first, who was close to needing life support. Just as she had asked, Gormon gave the patient a boost of his healing energy enough to pull them out of a downward spiral. Then he saw Nienna arrive as he moved to the next patient. Someone must have portaled her to Earth. As nearly everyone in the emergency department was sick, Stephanie had to point out the three with fae arrow poisoning. Within an hour the chaos stopped and almost everyone was well enough to be discharged. Gormon and Nienna healed the entire department including a few employees who were working with sore backs, high blood pressure, diabetes, or headaches. Then the two disappeared from her vision. She wondered if they went upstairs to the children's unit or returned to the Elven Republic. They had left quite a commotion in their wake.

One of the employees said, "Dr. Jones, can you work every shift with me? It was like a miracle swept through the department with all of the patients getting well. I thought for sure we were going to have a rash of deaths today. I was also in trouble when my glucose monitor showed my sugars start to spike, and that stopped as well. I've been maintaining a perfect range for several hours now and I didn't even do anything."

Stephanie smiled and said, "Some days we get lucky here and this must have been one of them. Congrats on your glucose control; if it keeps up, you should contact your physician to adjust your meds," Stephanie knew that if her colleague contacted her physician they would be confused by the disappearance of her diabetic symptoms.

Stephanie was happy for the employees who had been healed as well. She wondered how Gormon or Nienna had managed to catch the employees sitting still long enough to pour healing energy into them. Still, she understood that these employees had been lucky. Their lives were potentially extended by decades by eliminating their chronic illnesses. However, her elven healers didn't have the capacity to heal all of Earth's population. Nor would this planet handle the overpopulation that would result from everyone's illnesses being cured. She wondered if the healing energy worked into the future for the employees. Would they be unlikely to develop cancers that had been in their future? Would their blood sugars stabilize for days, weeks, or years? It was a question to ask when she visited the healers that evening.

She circled back to the three patients she was sure had been hit by poison arrows now that they were well enough to give a detailed story of where they had been. She needed to know where these bad fae were located so their small team could return them to the Elven Republic.

Stephanie was alarmed to learn that all three had been outside walking the dog, landscaping, or bike riding in her own suburb. She was alarmed as that meant the fae prisoners were moving out of a very sparsely populated area and into a highly populated area. She wondered if Gormon had some means to put a forcefield around witch area that the prisoners were likely located inside to keep them from harming humans. It would be something to strategize that evening. She also thought they had already removed the arrow-shooting fae from this world, but apparently not.

She was giving her report to her colleague taking over the

next shift. Once Gormon and Nienna had left, the emergency department again had sick patients who needed care. Still, it was a lighter load than usual. Each shift had at least two physicians, and the other physician on Stephanie's shift remarked what a miracle the shift had been. Patients they had thought would die hadn't and even had lived to be discharged with normal vital signs.

"Even my backache is gone. I was building a rock wall at home over the past few days and all the heavy lifting was tweaking me every time I moved. That's completely gone and I'm working the next few days, so hopefully the muscle soreness won't be coming back. Wasn't this an amazing shift, Stephanie?"

"It was. I've never seen anything like it. It's nice to have a breather every once in a while."

"I wonder if we should refer a review of our care to our quality nurse. Maybe she can figure out what we did differently to turn the tide for these patients," her colleague suggested.

"We could," Stephanie agreed. It would be interesting to see what statistical data would show after the elven healing. She was sure there would be no explanation other than everyone got well for unknown reasons.

They finished their report just as a rule-out myocardial infarction better known as a potential heart attack was rolling in. The new shift had work to do, and Stephanie wanted to go home. She was in her car and soon heading home in mild traffic. Tomorrow would be her last day of work before Amelia joined them for about ten days to hunt down these prisoners.

When she arrived home, Michael, Gormon, and Nienna were waiting for her. She wanted food, but she had lots to discuss with the three elves. She opted for delivery of Mexican food. She hoped that after the long day and adrenaline rush she had expended on the patients injured by the fae prisoners, the

Mexican food wouldn't make her fall asleep; but likely any big meal would do that. Besides, she would take a side trip with Michael to explain spices and spicy food.

With her order due to arrive in twenty minutes, she changed clothes and settled in for a conversation. She brought her scrubs out for Gormon to clean as she had iodine dye on them from earlier in the shift after she had thoroughly swabbed someone's wound with the substance.

"Nienna, in this world, healers come home with blood and other substances on their clothes after treating patients. It is really quite barbaric," Gormon said with elven superiority in his voice for the messy ways that humans healed.

"Hey, we were doing the best we can. Besides, don't your healers get dirty on occasion? Surely when you deliver a baby, there are all kinds of fluids that get on your healers."

"There are instances of fluids," Nienna said with a knowing smile. "Lord Mialynn has not witnessed a birth to understand that."

"Do your elven men usually witness the births of their children?"

"Some do. It's an evolving thought process in our realm," Nienna replied, with that same smile.

Both Gormon and Michael had wary looks on their faces. Like they knew there was a trap ahead for them and there was nothing they could do.

Stephanie let them off the hook and decided to talk about her concerns.

"First, thank you for healing both my patients and the staff. While I would love to have you do that every day, I realize that you're a limited resource and our planet is in danger of over-population. That said, there are already countries like Italy and Japan that are not having enough births to replace the deaths of their residents. It's creating an economic problem as there are not enough young people to pay into pension plans or even take care of their elders. We humans deteriorate as we grow older, unlike you elves."

The three elves looked at her as though she spoke a foreign language. So she said, "Never mind. Let's talk about the poison-filled arrows that are hitting humans in this area. I need to know what poison is being used. I don't like having to call you when humans are in trouble. The poison they're using must be something found on Earth as they can't be portaling back to your world to pick up materials, right?"

"Maybe. We can't track all possible portals in the Elven Republic, nor can all the prisoners use a portal. Most fae species can't portal."

"But Ramsey would have the ability to portal his followers, correct?"

"Yes. That's a possibility."

"So how do we find out what this poison is? I'm frustrated at my inability to save my people," Stephanie said.

"Did you collect any arrows today?"

"I did. I managed to find one on each patient. I went after it first thinking the longer the arrow was in, the more poison it might spread. Let me dig out the specimen cup from my purse and perhaps Nienna can tell me what the poison is," she said, handing the cup over to the healer.

Nienna initially wasn't sure what to do with the cup, so Michael showed her how to unscrew it. She opened the cup and sniffed it, and said, "This is a plant. I will check with a plant expert whom I know to identify it and tell us if it grows in both worlds."

"Not to be rude, but can you bring your expert to our meeting with the healers tonight as soon as we finish dinner? I have another shift tomorrow, so if I can counter the poison, that would be important," Stephanie said. The doorbell had just rung, signifying the delivery of their dinner.

Stephanie opened the cartons of food and explained the dishes, encouraging everyone to try a little of everything. Gormon sighed when his fellow elves showed enthusiasm for the food. It was a colorful display and not anything like the game he hunted while he was out on a mission. Nevertheless, he filled a plate as well, trying to understand Michael's and Nienna's enchantment with the flavors. He secretly admitted to himself that the food was delicious and perhaps this was one small thing that humans were better at than elves.

Stephanie cleaned up the detritus of their meal and was ready to portal to meet with the healers. It was an exciting thought as a physician to meet healers from another world. There would be the mystery of what was transferable between the two worlds. If she was keeping score, her Earth team was one ahead for the mouth-breathing technique she would teach the healers. If they could identify the poison, then that would even the score.

Until now, the only place she had seen was the palace. Now, she portaled to the elven version of a hospital.

Gormon indicated that Michael and he would be elsewhere in the Elven Republic and to have Nienna contact them when she was ready to return. The healer introduced Stephanie to her colleagues.

"Would it be rude of me to ask for us to do patient rounds on the fae you're treating here?"

"What are patient rounds?" One of the other healers asked.

"On Earth, we healers—or physicians, as we are called—learn through books and lectures and by something called patient rounds. A group of physicians, both experienced and new, walk around to each patient's room and discuss their case. It's a way to learn and to have more than one brain considering each case. 'Patient' is the word we call humans whom a physician is caring for in an office or hospital. A hospital is where we care for patients."

The healers nodded and they walked to the first room. "This is a dwarf who was injured while crafting a sword for the king's army. He suffered a deep wound to his foot when he accidentally dropped it. As he had imbued the sword with magic, it was strong and sharp, nearly severing his foot. With the dwarf's own healing magic as well as two of our healers, we were able to rebuild the foot. Now he's staying off his foot until it heals completely in another day."

"Do you worry about infection?" Stephanie asked.

"No, we rinsed the foot before we performed any magic."

"So you didn't have to give him any herbs or plants to prevent an infection from occurring?" Stephanie asked.

The healers looked puzzled and asked, "What is this infection you speak of?"

"In the human world, avoiding an infection is a big deal. Humans react to foreign bacteria. They run a fever, produce pus, and can die. We treat infections with something called antibiotics. The first antibiotic discovered by our healers was penicillin nearly one hundred years ago. It greatly reduced the death rate of our warriors in a bad war that occurred on Earth. It's a type of mold that blocks the enzymes that bacterial cells need to replicate."

Stephanie looked around at the healers, who looked politely confused at her explanation. It was time to change tactics. "Let's continue," Stephanie said as she quickly realized that talking human science with these healers was a nonstarter.

She saw fae species in various stages of healing, then they moved on to a room to have a discussion. She wished they had conference rooms like this on Earth. You felt healed just walking into it. The room was bathed in ethereal, soft light;

emanating from luminescent crystals suspended in the air. The walls were adorned with delicate vines and flowers that seemed to glow with an otherworldly energy. The floor was covered in a carpet of lush, iridescent moss, creating a soothing and natural ambiance.

In the center of the room, a circular pool of shimmering water reflected the healing energy that filled the space. Floating orbs of light hovered above, emitting a gentle hum. Enchanted butterflies flitted about, leaving trails of sparkling dust in their wake. The furniture was crafted from intertwined branches and adorned with healing herbs and flowers. Plush cushions made of enchanted petals provided comfortable seating for the fae healers. Stephanie stood at the entrance, enchanted. She fantasized about their emergency room waiting room looking like this to soothe patients and their families. Then abruptly like an old record being scratched on a turntable, she imagined humans in the room vomiting or having diarrhea and realized the room would stay clean for about thirty seconds. Oh well.

"What were you thinking, Dr. Jones?" Nienna asked, having seen this human healer go somewhere else for a moment.

"Do the fae vomit or get food poisoning and have diarrhea?"

The healers looked perplexed.

So, she imitated the movement of throwing up.

The healers smiled and shook their heads.

"The fae all have some basic ability to heal themselves starting with the distress you mention. If the fae can't do it for themselves if they are too young, then any other fae can do it for them."

"This is a marvelous room that we are meeting in, and for a minute or two I was imagining it in a human hospital. Then I saw my patients vomiting in this beautiful space and decided it would never work." She pointed at the crystals and asked, "What do you use crystals for? I haven't seen you use one on Earth."

"When we have a particularly difficult case, our healers may need reviving, and both the pool and the crystals do that for us."

"Ah. As you know, we have zero use of magic in our healing on Earth. We use science and technology that has evolved over the centuries. I've had to treat Gormon a few times after encountering your prisoners. I've performed mouth to mouth, a technique my daughter and I will teach you after we collect all the prisoners."

Nienna gently interrupted, "One moment, Dr. Jones. I'm going to give my fellow healers an image of what you were doing."

There was silence in the room and then she watched as the healers' eyes went wide and landed on her.

"We do that, and something called cardiac resuscitation where we pump on someone's chest to restart the heart. Together the two techniques are called CPR. We do this until we can use drugs or electricity to jumpstart someone's heart. We also stick a breathing tube down their throat to breathe for them until they can do so on their own. It likely sounds crude compared to your magic, but we save thousands of lives on Earth with that technique."

"It does sound crude, but I've learned in my brief interactions with your world that your healers do a lot of good without magic."

"What I want to know now is some science about the fae. I've had to rescue Gormon twice now. In humans, we breathe twelve times a minute. With elves, how many times do you breathe each minute? How many times does your heart beat each minute? I won't worry about body temperature as you don't get infections. Also, eventually when we teach CPR, we'll need to know the sizes of your species so we can bring the right equipment."

"I do not know how fast our heart beats or how many breaths we take, but we will learn. I do not understand your question about size. Can you explain?" asked one of the healers.

"We humans carry equipment in our emergency transportation. Remember, we can't portal to heal the person; the person needs to come to us. We send something called an ambulance to treat and bring to our hospital people who need our care in an emergency. The size of a human infant's mouth is much smaller than an adult's. Thus, we have masks to fit the different-sized mouths. Gormon mentioned that he sent a giant back home from the prison. I don't know if you're called to save giants or if all giants are considered monsters and therefore you don't heal them. If you do want to care for them, you'll need different-sized equipment."

"You've given us a lot to think about. I especially liked your idea of 'rounds' where we can exchange information. I have two other comments for you. My plant expert studied the arrow and said the plant was a belladonna plant, which grows on Earth as well as here, so we have no way of knowing where the plant came from. Also, we wondered if we might be able to teach you some witch healing." Nienna said.

# Chapter Sixteen

"You're able to teach me witch healing? Wow, of course I want to learn! Belladonna is a plant on Earth, but the prisoners wouldn't find the plant inside the forest they're situated in as it's too cold to grow there at the moment. So either they flitted around Earth to a warmer climate to get it or they portaled back to your realm."

"Hmmm, I hadn't thought of it being too cold to grow the belladonna plant, but that makes sense. Maybe I can have our plant expert do a few more experiments to determine the source of the plant."

"Yes, the location is important. Whether they have portaled around Earth or to here is of concern."

Nienna nodded and stayed still while she had a telepathic conversation with someone else. It was really unnerving not to be able to eavesdrop on conversations.

"Okay, let's teach you some of our healing skills."

Stephanie was both awed and suspicious. She had seen the healers save humans through their touch. However, she was steeped in western medicine and couldn't believe that she could have a healing touch. If she could learn, she would be the best physician ever.

"How about if we start by using your healing touch to stop or reduce pain? It will take a while to teach you this. I don't think you'll learn much in a single session. But I believe you can learn because you have magical blood as evidenced by the grimoire," Nienna said.

Stephanie nodded, but she wondered if she would have much use for reducing pain in the hospital. Yes, she saw many patients with pain throughout her shifts in the emergency department, but her behavior would be considered freaky by colleagues and patients alike. Most would probably wonder if she was praying over patients. Still, if all she could do was eliminate her own occasional aches and pains, that would be a win.

Nienna held out her hands with her fingers splayed. "When I approach someone to heal, my fingers feel the channels of pain or damage inside the body."

Stephanie tamped down her feelings of "oh boy, this is woo-woo bullcrap" and tried to follow the healer.

"The person you're healing must give something back to the universe. I don't have unlimited power to heal as any healing reduces my energy."

"Yes, I saw that when Gormon healed an entire unit of sick children. He was exhausted afterward."

"Exactly, and it works to a large degree the same way in the human world."

"It does?" asked Stephanie.

"Yes. I've seen you breathe for Gormon. Could you do that for a long period of time?"

"No. I would be too exhausted. I see what you mean, though, with that example. However, when I breathed for

Gormon, he was not voluntarily giving something back. His mind was gone because he was too ill to supply energy to his brain. How do you handle someone's agreement that they will give something back to the world?"

"In the fae world you understand that is the trade-off to balance the universe."

"So how about someone like Ramsey—would you heal him?"

"It is not for me to judge. I will save everyone. If they don't give back, the universe will turn on them eventually. Ramsey has spent two centuries in prison. That's quite a loss of personal freedom," Nienna said.

"Yes, but when he was released from that prison, he began his plan to take over Earth, and harm humans, so how is the universe striking back now?" Stephanie asked.

"It will strike back. It may not happen in your lifetime, but it will happen. We fae have absolute confidence that payback will occur."

"We have a saying on Earth—karma is a bitch, or you get what you give. It sounds like your feelings are the elven equivalent of that philosophy."

"Perhaps. Let's go back to your breathing for Gormon. How did you know you needed to do that?"

"In human medicine, we know that it's most important to keep the brain filled with oxygen and the heart and lungs are what do that; therefore, we always check those things first. So, when I arrived at his side, I brought a stethoscope and could tell his heart was beating, but his lungs were not moving air. You can't continue to live very long without breathing. Thus, my daughter and I breathed for him until he could do so himself."

"We healers put our hands on something and feel vibration or signals that tell us where the problem is, and we then seek to draw out the bad essence, so to speak," Nienna said.

Stephanie nodded, though she had no idea what the healer was talking about. Nienna cut her arm with a dagger. It wasn't a deep cut, but it proceeded to bleed. She held her arm to Stephanie and said, "Put your hands on my arm and see if you can feel the pain of the cut."

Stephanie had seen pictures of old surgery rooms and equipment, and this made her feel like she was participating in some prehistoric torture. Still, she concentrated with her eyes closed, as Nienna instructed, searching for any kind of channel or whisper of pain or injury she could feel. Instead, there was nothing. Finally, she opened her eyes and looked up at Nienna and said, "I couldn't feel anything. Maybe you need fae blood to be a healer."

Nienna held up her arm and the wound was completely healed.

Stephanie looked at it and said, "Is that your elven self-healing?"

"No, that was you."

"I'm sorry. I don't believe you. I think you healed yourself."

"I would not lie to you, Dr. Jones," Nienna said, with offense in her voice.

"You're a generous person, Nienna. I'm sure you would want to credit me with healing, but I didn't feel anything like what you described. I'll try it tomorrow at work if I have the chance."

"Well okay. We will work on measurements for you of how much we breathe and how often our hearts beat. We will be ready when you and your daughter are ready to teach us. Gormon is waiting outside this room to portal you to Earth."

"Thank you for an extraordinary evening, and I look forward to many more exchanges of knowledge and techniques. I noticed you have herbs and crystals and probably other things that I might duplicate on Earth. Also, thank you for identifying the plant. I'll be able to counteract that the next time I see a patient with that injury, and I won't need to call on you or Gormon for help."

The healers nodded and Stephanie and Nienna went to where Gormon was waiting to open a portal back to Earth. Stephanie blinked and was soon in her kitchen. She looked at the clock and was surprised that the hour with Nienna had actually been three hours. She guessed that time flew when you liked what you were doing. Suddenly, she felt exhaustion hit as it had been a long day followed by the visit to the healers. The next day was her last shift for a while. She'd taken off the following week to coincide with her daughter's college break. They would spend the next week hunting for prisoners instead. Amelia would drive home after wrapping up her last exam and be home in time for dinner.

"What's your plan for tomorrow?" Stephanie asked.

"Michael and I will go after a few more prisoners on the list. A small group of warriors is also meeting with Skar to discuss the weapons we need created for the upcoming battle with Ramsey."

"Do you think this battle will be different because it will be on Earth compared to your previous battle, or is there a way to do a broad portal and take them back as a group to your realm for the fight?"

"We do not have a group portal, but remember, you must willingly walk through it."

"Have you performed a magic signal exploration to find Ramsey and his followers? I would think it would be an especially strong signal with so many people."

"I have performed that test and I do believe I know where they are located."

"Have they stayed in one place or are they moving around?

It's cold at this time of year near Lake Tahoe. Besides the fairy you returned earlier to your world, are any of the fae prisoners susceptible to cold? I've noticed you don't seem to be. We humans put on more and bulkier clothes near the snow."

"We have charms that control for too much heat or cold. Ramsey would be able to control the temperature for his followers. Still, I would guess that they have shelter."

"So perhaps they've taken over some kind of building?"

"I am not sure."

"Can you show me on a map where they are?"

"I will need to take your map with me when Michael and I are in the area tomorrow so I can provide you with a more exact location."

"Of the fewer than forty prisoners still on the loose, how many are alone or in a small group versus how many are with Ramsey?"

"I am getting a signal that two are not even in this area."

"How far away are they?" Stephanie asked, alarmed that the prisoners were spreading out.

"I do not know how to describe distance in your world," Gormon said. "My sense is the distance from here to where we have been collecting prisoners would equal perhaps one hundred times the distance to where we will find these other prisoners."

"Okay, that's about ten thousand miles. How would they get that far away? Did they fly or portal or swim or run?"

"Swim?"

Stephanie pulled up a video of an Olympic swimmer in the pool.

"Oh. No to swimming or walking. I do not know for sure who these two prisoners are, but some prisoners on my list have wings and would therefore be capable of flying."

After her encounter with the two aquatic monsters at Lake Tahoe, it was good to know there was not some kind of shark or whale that was somehow on land but could also swim fast in the ocean.

"How many prisoners on your list have portal capabilities, and are all portal capabilities the same? Does it take less skill or energy to portal around Earth than to portal to the Elven Republic?"

"We do not portal around Earth. We portal back to the Elven Republic and then to a new location on Earth. It is so quick you would not notice it."

"So that leads to the question of does the Elven Republic notice these quick bounces of portals? Did Cellica indicate which of the prisoners have portal abilities?" Stephanie asked, looking at her written list and scanning for the word. "I don't see it listed anywhere, but we were more focused on understanding how they would fight us or defend themselves. Maybe we didn't ask the portal question."

Gormon nodded and said, "I will head there overnight and speak to her. It is interesting when you look at the portal powers of our fae species. Cellica is a moon witch and cannot portal, nor can our healers even though they are elves, so maybe there is not one answer for each species."

"That is interesting. Perhaps Nienna has put all her power into healing and never learned to divert her magic into creating portals. How did you learn to portal?"

Gormon paused to think back over his long life and just shook his head. "I have lived a long time, and I cannot remember when I first learned to portal."

"Wow, I hadn't thought about all the space in your memory for over three hundred years of living. I don't remember much of my life before age five or six, and I feel like I've lived through a lot of experiences since then. I can't imagine my brain storing millions of images. Heck, I can't even imagine what my photo storage would be like. It's a good thing you fae don't have cameras."

"What is a camera?"

Stephanie pulled out her cell phone, opened the camera app, hit the button for a selfie, then moved next to Gormon and took their picture. Then she looked at the camera and laughed at the result—Gormon had looked suspicious when she moved next to him and aimed her phone at the two of them. So, she showed him the picture.

"This might be one of the most amazing things I have seen on Earth. As much as we do not want the fae world changed by Earth or its technology, this camera is special. I will share it with the king later."

"Just a moment," Stephanie said, as she dashed to her bedroom and gathered up different photos of Amelia.

"With our camera technology, we can keep photos electronically on our phones or we can print them on special paper like this," she said, laying out five different photos of Amelia at various ages. "This is Amelia at ages two, five, eight, fifteen, and eighteen. I will have pictures of my daughter at various ages forever."

Gormon studied the pictures, fascinated with both the technology and seeing a human move through various ages. Then Stephanie left the room again and came back with a sheet of paper that had their selfie picture printed on it.

"Here, you can share this with your king," Stephanie said, giving the paper to Gormon.

"I will. Thank you."

They said their goodnights and Stephanie headed to bed, while Gormon returned to his world with more questions than ever to get answered. When he was first assigned the duty of collecting their realm's prisoners, he envisioned using his portal power to pick off one after another. He would use his swords where necessary, and he would have them all collected by now, including Ramsey. This had turned into a far more interesting and slower mission than he ever predicted.

# Chapter Seventeen

amsey was looking around at the small structure he'd taken over. It had been deserted and according to a sign on the door was scheduled for demolition soon. The sign said it would be the end of April, but he had no idea of what April meant. He'd been quick to act when he was released from the suspended-animation prison. He'd realized it was likely a magical malfunction as no one was immediately there to stop them from leaving. The fools had sent him to prison with his wand. He wondered how much time had passed—was it short or long? As both the Elven Republic and Earth revolved around the same moon and sun, their passage of time was similar. However, he had found no markers of time that he recognized. Still, he'd seen technology here and more people than the Earth in which he'd been imprisoned years ago. At first, he thought the Earthlings had magic as he had seen lights everywhere—bright lights that were more than candles could generate. Between the lights and the moving contraptions, they had advanced without magic.

When the suspended-animation died, all the prisoners

came alive. They could see the sky through the mountain top and some of those who could fly or climb or teleport left the cavern before he'd had a chance to convince them to join his team. In the end, he walked away with about thirty followers. It helped that the prisoners were slow to come to awareness. Some of the prisoners were his followers from when he tried to take over the Elven Republic. He'd come so close before the king's warriors captured him and sent him to this awful prison. At least he had the satisfaction of killing the king before his capture. Now he was free. He had initially planned another attempt on the Elven Republic, but as he led his group of followers away from the prison, he was impressed with the technology he saw humans using in this world. He had big dreams of combining his magic with this world's technology.

That said, given Ramsey powers, it would be easy to take over an Earth that has no magic or magical beings. He just needed a good plan and some magical followers to help him. He wondered in the beginning if the Elven Republic noticed that the suspended animation failed. He'd thought about just hiding here on Earth, but then some of his fellow prisoners were unsure what to do and where to go and he quickly changed his plans. Still, he knew they needed to leave the cavern and he set about doing that with his followers. He was the first warlock in the history of the fae to kill a king.

Some of his followers were happy to find shelter as they were cold. He'd had to cast a warming spell to keep them warm and engaged as they moved through the snow to their present location. He'd also recognized a few of the monsters from his prison and had quickly placed them where they could do the greatest damage to humans. It had been easy to cast a spell to move them from the cavern to a nearby body of water. He'd been happy to watch the giant climb out by himself. When he left with his followers, there were still another fifty or so prisoners that he'd been unable to convince to join with him. He assumed in time the Elven Republic would discover the prison failed and send someone to retrieve those prisoners. Whatever, he hadn't cared what happened to them as they had made the bad decision not to follow him. He had since registered the presence of a strong magical signal in distant lands, and thought it was likely that the Elven Republic knew of the prison break and was after him and his followers.

As he studied the group that followed him, he looked for two leaders whom he could plan with and who could lead small groups to help in the takeover of Earth. Also, he knew he needed a map to understand where they were and where he wanted to mount his attack from. He knew parts of Earth had kings and other parts had presidents or premiers. He remembered the history lessons his parents delivered before they had met an early death.

Apparently, parts of this world took a survey of people and that's how they were elected. He was the only warlock sentenced to that prison and was the most powerful magic user of his group, and indeed in the Elven Republic. No single king's warrior could defeat him. Combining his thought processes with his skills would make him a powerful leader in no time. Surely, as he looked at the thirty fae around him, he had early proof of his theory. He'd watched two of his followers from his previous battle against the king for the past couple of moon changes and decided they would fit the bill. They were good magic users and would follow his directions. He motioned them to follow him to another room so he could talk over his plans.

"I want to start planning our takeover of this world. I'd like you two to assist me."

They nodded eagerly. Daggo was larger than Ramsey, he was a half-elf, half-orc. His skin had a slight green tint, and unlike most orcs he didn't have his bottom teeth appearing above his upper lip. He had a headful of hair and visage that looked fierce. Enda was a female half-elf half-goblin. She had a mottled complexion and sharp teeth but had the usual pointed ears and strong features of elves. She carried a couple of daggers on her person and had a look of cunning. Ramsey recognized that look as he often had the same expression when he glanced into a mirror.

"I think the first thing we need to do is map out this planet. Where are we? We'll need to know where the big cities are located so we can make our plan to dominate them."

"Don't you think we are near a big city? It seemed like there were a lot of people moving about in those machines."

"I don't know. We need to find out how long we were in that prison. Perhaps the Earth's population grew. Do you have any idea of how to find that number?"

"I could try portaling home and ask someone what year it is," Enda said. "My cousin felt bad when I was sent to prison, so she wouldn't snitch on me by telling the king's people that I was in the Elven Republic.

"That's a good suggestion. Would you try that, Enda, once we conclude our meeting? Does either of you know someone back home who has a map of this world? I don't recall ever seeing one. I just remember there were many kings and presidents here," Ramsey said.

"Maybe ask someone else in our group if they know what Earth looks like. It will make them feel good if they know the answer," Daggo said.

Ramsey nodded. "That's an excellent idea. We don't have to solve everything ourselves. I'd also like to start training everyone in magical power. It will give them purpose and get them ready for our coming invasion. Let's start with a few basic magic spells—invisibility and a protection bubble. From there, let's talk about magical weapons and who can use what."

Daggo and Enda nodded in agreement and Enda asked, "How should we split them up? I can work with any species."

"Then we'll divide them into two equal groups after you return from the Elven Republic with the answer to our question. While you're gone, we'll talk with the group."

Ramsey had the tiniest worry that once she portaled home, she wouldn't come back, but she would be imprisoned again in the Elven Republic and in this world they could run free. He gathered his followers together for a meeting.

"Let's gather and discuss our plans. I've named Daggo and Enda as my assistants. Enda has portaled back to our realm to find out how long we were in that wretched prison. We need to know that to help us understand what's happened in this world. We've all been able to see the use of technology in this world. It's like the goblin race infused it. Enda and Daggo will also be dividing you into two groups to practice skills we'll need for the coming battle. From here on out let's use the following titles. I'm Arch Warlock Ramsey and they are Colonel Daggo and Colonel Enda. We'll add additional titles as necessary. For me to plan our takeover of this world, we need a little more knowledge about it. Is anyone able to draw a map of Earth so that we may figure out where we are and where we want to attack?"

One of the followers spoke up and said "There's an old map in one of the rooms. I don't know if it is accurate as I don't remember my lessons about Earth."

"Bring it to me. It may be a starting place," Ramsey said, as Enda reappeared next to him.

"We've been locked up for just over two hundred years," Enda said in a low voice to Ramsey. She was shocked at being forgotten by their people. It reinforced her desire to help

Ramsey take over this world. How dare her homeland forget about her for so long.

Her words served to cause anger and despair over the waste of time in that prison. No one could think of anyone who had been sentenced to two hundred years of prison. It also served to unite Ramsey's followers once he repeated her answer out loud. There was instant conversation as discussions occurred at being forgotten and wondering who among their relatives were still alive. While the elven race was nearly immortal, several other followers' species were not so lucky, and they had lost a generation or two of family. Ramsey was an elf, so it didn't matter that he'd lost two hundred years. Besides, he'd long ago been cast out by his family after he adopted dark magic.

The person who mentioned the map returned with a dusty map. When they arrived at this building, there had been dirt and dust on every surface. Ramsey had cast a spell to clean up most of it and then set forth providing heat, light, bedding, and food for his followers. Now he studied the map. He could only hope that the star on the map was an indication of where they were presently located. He vaguely remembered being told he was being sent to a mountainous region on Earth. The map had squiggly marks which he took to mean mountain peaks. It showed a large lake between two areas designated as "California" and "Nevada." It appeared as though they were located in the United States of America. He assumed that each state was governed by a king or president.

"We'll start planning on taking over California and then we'll spread out taking over more of these states," Ramsey said to the cheers of his followers. "This world appears larger than the Elven Republic and likely has more than one king. So we'll conquer one island at a time. This island appears large and will prove to the remainder of the Earth that we are powerful. It looks as though there are enough islands and more for each of us to become territorial rulers. I need to plan our invasion with Daggo and Enda, and meanwhile you need to practice your magical skills and the building of weapons."

Ramsey looked around the room at his followers. They were all charged with some crime, and he would have to worry about someone in his group of followers trying to overpower him. That was the nature of this group, but he had no worries about the outcome as he was the strongest warlock the Elven Republic had ever seen. It was why he'd been sent to such a horrible off-realm prison and forgotten about for two centuries. Still, he would use that circumstance to keep his followers motivated and angry.

"One final note: I've sensed magical signals besides our own here. The numbers have diminished, including the Aboleth and Merrow that were in Lake Tahoe. Either the humans have figured out a way to kill them or they've been portaled back to the Elven Republic. I believe there's at least one warrior here collecting prisoners. With all of us located in one space, we're probably a beacon to that warrior. As we think that there aren't mountains everywhere, I would like to move us closer to a city on this map called Sacramento. It has a star by it, so perhaps that's the location of the palace. It will be warmer there and there will be more people, but it will likely put us closer to that warrior. Still, I can defeat any warrior by myself. I tell you this so you don't relax your guard. You may be tempted to leave this location and explore, but as I have revealed my plans to all of you, know that I will end the life of anyone who leaves the group now."

Ramsey had given his followers a lot of things to think about their current situation. He thought he had both motivated them and scared them, but also offered hope for a kingdom somewhere of their own on this planet. He was going to leave his two assistants in charge and go explore so there would be no surprises when they designed their campaign to take over California and then the United States. He also wanted to evaluate the magic signature he was detecting—he would go observe the area to collect information on his opponents. He was a little worried that he might underestimate technology as a counter to magic, but he was smart and powerful and could overcome anything with a little planning.

# Chapter Eighteen

Stephanie left for work that next morning. She was looking forward to her daughter's arrival later that day, though she worried about the danger facing the two of them. She made it through half of her busy shift before she had the chance to try what Nienna had tried to teach her the previous night. She had someone come in for pain management. Sadly, she was dying from cancer. The patient already had some morphine on board. That took the edge off excruciating pain, but Stephanie wanted to know if she could do more. The patient was resting, and Stephanie offered to sit with her for a few minutes to see what else she could do. Her worst pain was coming from her thigh bone—the femur. It was one of numerous places where her bone cancer had spread. They would likely send her to radiation medicine as they could achieve pain reduction through radiation.

Stephanie sat down and placed her hands on the woman's thigh, jokingly saying, "I've been told my hands have the healing touch. Let me see if I can ease your pain a bit more than the powerful drugs we've given you."

She searched for that whisper of pain and imagined pulling it out of the patient's body. A short time later, the patient whispered, "Either the drugs went into hyper speed, or you do have healing hands. My pain is gone. Thank you."

"Really? I thought my co-workers were just being kind."

"My pain is gone. How did you do that? Can you teach my family members? Do you think it will come back?" the patient said.

Stephanie was feeling panicky over the patient's expectations. She felt proud to have accomplished something for the woman and yet distraught that she was unable to teach the woman's family how to heal her pain.

"It was just dumb luck on my part. Tell your family to put their hands on whatever part of your body is in pain and imagine wisps of pain leaving your body and floating away. Actually, don't tell them that as it will cause them and others to doubt my competence as a physician. As to whether your pain will come back, I can't say. I didn't shrink your tumor or anything, so I don't know what to tell you," Stephanie said, backing out of the room.

She moved onto other patients, still shaken by the effect she'd had on the cancer patient. It made no medical or scientific sense. She had a sense of unease for the remainder of her shift. She was happy with herself for easing the patient's pain, which was sort of the goal for centuries of medicine. However, she had never tried something unproven on another human until today, and that was a bad practice even though she'd done nothing invasive with medication, devices, or surgery. Had she physically altered a patient's body with her care? She'd thought about ordering an Xray to see if she had shrunk the size of the tumor, but her colleagues would look upon that as unnecessary care. It was only relevant if the patient was going to radiation medicine and instead, with her pain under control, she'd been discharged home. She vowed not to try her healing-hands experiment again until she understood it better.

The shift was coming to an end and her colleagues would be there soon for her to report to; then she had nearly ten days of blissful time off in which to hunt monsters that might hurt humans. An hour later she was pulling into her garage and found her daughter's car was already inside. She walked inside and hugged Amelia asking, "How did your exams go?"

"I aced them. I just checked, and the scores were posted by the time I arrived here. My lowest score was an 85 in organic chemistry, but I had higher scores through the semester, so I'll end up with an A-."

"I remember that being a hard class and I don't recall what my final exam grade was, but I would be happy for an A-."

"Where are Michael and Gormon?"

"I don't know. Are they in the house meditating?" Stephanie asked, though her experience with them had them appearing in her kitchen as soon as she arrived home.

"I don't think so; just a minute and I'll look." She came back to the kitchen and said, "No one is here but us."

"Perhaps they're out collecting prisoners. I'll text them."

She did so and then went to her bedroom to change while she was waiting to hear from them. By the time she returned to the kitchen, both men had returned.

"What did you guys achieve today?" Stephanie asked.

"We returned three more prisoners to the Elven Republic. We also spied on Ramsey. I believe spy is the right human word," Gormon said, with Michael nodding.

"Wow, that's a big deal. How did you get close and where is he?"

"He and his followers—perhaps thirty of them—are staying in an abandoned structure. There's a sign out front that says, "Lakeside Inn," but it appears to be closed. There's a sign on the door that says it is scheduled for demolition in April. I do not when that is."

"We use a twelve-month calendar in most of this world. It's called the Gregorian calendar. We are currently in the month of March and April is next month. This is the fifteenth day out of a possible thirty-one days. A day is twenty-four hours in which the sun rises and sets, and darkness takes over. There are other calendars in use for religious or other reasons, but the vast majority of the world uses the Gregorian calendar. If the notice says April, the demolition could be between sixteen and forty-six days from now, as April has thirty days."

Gormon nodded and said, "Okay, then he is going to have to move on. With no money and thirty followers, he will need a large empty building. That area he is in currently feels much less crowded than the city you work in. Is that correct?"

"Yes, it's a tiny city compared to where I work. I'm worried that he might be rash and show his magic to the human world, not caring about your ancient pact to keep humans ignorant of the Elven Republic. While we don't have magic, we have guns and bombs that will kill any fae. He won't be taking over any part of Earth, but if you want to quietly recover these prisoners, let's hope Ramsey doesn't do anything rash.

"If that happens, our mission will change. Depending how bad his exposure is will determine our response. We actually have a mind wipe ability within our realm. Even if Ramsey exposes the human world to his behavior, we can block it from the minds of humans."

"Gormon, you're wrong. Your mind-wipe thing won't work here on Earth," Amelia said, holding up her phone. "Nearly everyone on Earth carries these phones around and they have the ability to take pictures or videos of anything at any time. Then we have this thing called social media where we can upload our photos and videos and share them with the rest of the world. Someone doing magic would be captured on screen and shared with millions of humans before the Elven Republic could stop it. Let me demonstrate it."

Amelia took a short video of her mother's family room. Then she uploaded it to TikTok after explaining what TikTok was and the ideal of a video going viral. For the first time, Gormon rubbed his head and lost his usual haughty expression at the enormity of the problem of keeping magic a secret on Earth. In the end he said, "Michael and I must leave and discuss this situation with our fellow warriors and king. Amelia, would you mind coming with us for a demonstration of your phone's ability? If that is okay with you, Stephanie?"

Stephanie knew her daughter was an adult and would be thrilled with the opportunity to visit the Elven Republic. It was not an unsafe place so there was no risk, and she nodded her agreement.

"Before we go, let me capture you guys doing magic to drive home my point. Can you do a few things like clean mom's clothes, open a portal and walk through it in the backyard, and turn your invisibility spell on and off?" Amelia asked.

"Amelia, before you do that, let's talk about the danger of that. Can you put your phone on airplane mode, so it doesn't connect with a server anywhere, and then delete the videos before you turn your airplane mode off? We don't want any record of our magic on our phones for our own safety."

"Good point, Mom. I have a good friend at college who is a computer geek. Let me run it by him. Of course, I won't tell him why."

Stephanie nodded and watched her daughter sit down to text someone. Minutes later she had her answer that her Mom's suggestion would work if she also deleted the videos from her trash before she connected back to the network. Then they set up the three demonstrations of magic and recorded them on her phone. Michael and Gormon found it jarring to watch themselves on video.

"I do not like this video," Gormon said.

"Well, it's too late to do anything about it on Earth. We record everything. I have videos of most of Amelia's birthday parties and significant milestones in her life. Remember those Star Trek episodes? Those are shot with a camera, and we probably have millions of movies and TV shows worldwide. See you three later."

Gormon opened a portal and the three of them went to the Elven Republic. Stephanie took a seat on her couch, leaned back, and closed her eyes to think. She knew her daughter would have the time of her life visiting the realm and explaining the technology to them. Once they recaptured all of the prisoners, she wondered what they would do long-term keeping the lines of communication open between the two men and herself and her daughter. She admitted that meeting these elves was a life-changing event.

Her thoughts went back to her day at work and her effort at easing the cancer patient's pain. If she indeed has developed a healer's touch, how would she deploy it in her work? Further, what was the consequence of doing that? Magic was not unlimited, and in theory it took something away from her to use it. She thought back to when the patient said her pain was gone; how had she felt at that moment? She was both exhausted and elated. So maybe that was her answer. It was a mystery that would take time to solve. There were other spells she could learn from the grimoire, and there was the mystery of how the grimoire had ended up in her possession in the first place. So much to think about and do. Then she opened her eyes and thought about dinner. Should she plan food for all of them or would they eat in the palace? She decided it was easier to make dinner for all of them and leave herself with leftovers.

She was in the midst of cooking when a figure appeared in front of her. It was one she hadn't seen before. She briefly wondered if this was someone from the Elven Republic coming to collect her to join the other three. Then she decided that Gormon would have come himself. So who was this and what weapons did she have nearby? She would have wondered if this was simply someone breaking in, but the unusual clothes suggested that was not the case. She wondered if this was their nemesis, Ramsey. His skin was very light and his hair dark. He wore dark robes and carried a wand in his hand. He was handsome in his own way, but maybe it was impossible to be a warlock and be ugly.

Instead she asked, "Who are you?"

Her question was met with, "Who are you?"

She gave a childish response of, "I asked you first."

Ramsey looked at the woman, trying to figure her out. When he portaled where he was detecting a large magic signal, he expected to portal away quickly when he found a few warriors; instead, he met this calm human woman. He quickly recalculated his response.

"You don't seem surprised to meet me or shocked at my sudden appearance."

She picked up a knife and replied, "Actually, if you don't tell me who you are, I'll call the police and defend myself with a knife."

"Hmmm," was all he said, looking around.

Stephanie felt like a deer caught in the headlights. She thought this might be Ramsey, and if he'd killed a fae king, he could surely kill her. She decided to try an invisibility spell and then run out of the house with her cell phone and knife in hand. She wondered if she might get a picture of the man before she did that. So, she held her phone up, then snapped a picture. Then she decided to use her car rather than run away on foot. She started the engine with her app and even opened the garage door thanks to another app.

She deployed the invisibility spell while the man didn't have direct eyesight on her and moved out the door to her garage. She got in her car and reversed out of the driveway. She knew the man could follow her and land in the seat beside her if he wanted, but the way he was looking around her house made her think that he was looking for the presence of Gormon and Michael. She hoped he would just go away and she further hoped that Gormon and Michael wouldn't return while he was still there. She didn't want her house destroyed by a battle of the elves. She got a few miles away, pulled to the side of the road, and opened her security app to see if the man was still in her house. Unless he was in the bathroom, he had left her house. She watched a little longer and nothing was stirring. Granted, some of the rooms were dark as the lights hadn't been turned on, but she couldn't find him. She sighed and hoped he wouldn't appear on the seat next to her at any moment.

She remembered how to communicate with Gormon across the two worlds and sent him a message about what had happened. She nearly had a heart attack when he and Michael portaled to just outside of her car. As opposed to her house, portaling inside the car required a seated position. She unlocked the doors, and they climbed inside.

"You guys gave me a fright on top of the fright I just had. Whoever the person inside of my house was, since they were an elf, I was sure they could also pop up next to my car." She held her phone out to Gormon and asked, "Is this Ramsey? He never introduced himself. Where's Amelia?" Stephanie asked, hand still over her heart at the last few breathtaking moments.

"Maybe it was a relative of Spock's?" Michael said from the back seat. He'd learned that humans liked humor during stressful periods.

At that comment, Stephanie relaxed and smiled, "Thanks, Michael. Indeed, maybe it was a relative of Spock's."

"Yes, this is Ramsey. We left Amelia behind in case we had a battle when we arrived here. I will go retrieve her now that I know the situation is safe," Gormon said.

"Thank you, Gormon, from the bottom of my heart for looking out for my daughter. That means the world to me."

He nodded gravely and disappeared, and before she had time to ask Michael questions, he reappeared with Amelia outside of the car. Stephanie exited the car and gave her daughter a tight hug before returning to her car.

"What happened, Mom?"

"I apparently met Ramsey when he showed up at the house. I was pulling out ingredients to cook dinner and he appeared. I asked him who he was, and he asked me who I was. I told him he had to go first as I had asked first." That got a chuckle out of Amelia. "Then he said I was calm at his appearance, and I brandished a knife and said I was going to call the police and defend myself with it. He didn't seem worried and began looking around the house. So, I used the apps on my phone to open the garage door and start the car, and while I wasn't in his direct line of vision. I used the invisibility spell and got into the car and hightailed it out of there. Then I contacted Gormon, and I just checked the interior cameras and I don't see that he is still in the house," Stephanie said breathlessly.

"Wow, that was quick thinking on your part."

"Yeah, I'm quite proud of myself. However, I didn't try the protection spell. I don't know if it would have worked against him. I got the feeling he was surprised to meet a human. I just drove here hoping he couldn't pop into the seat next to me."

"We can't portal into a moving object. Ramsey might have tried, but the portal would take him to the last place you were located. We can portal a moving object, but not the reverse. Driving away from your house was the best possible way to protect yourself," Gormon said.

"Would he assume I was just a human; would he think I was a mixed species, or would he have known I used an invisibility spell? Do you have witches in the Elven Republic?"

Gormon smiled at her range of questions. He enjoyed her inquisitive mind and her quick thinking, "That is a good question. Michael, can you tell that Stephanie is a human? I can, but I do not know if that is a common trait."

Michael thought about the question and shook his head. "I don't seem to have the ability that you have to sense what kind of species is in front of me. I would know she's not an elf by her ears, but only by her clothes would I know she's not from our world."

Stephanie smiled about her clothing choices. From her two visits to the Elven Republic, she realized that they seemed to like more flowing garments. To her the garments would get in the way of care in the hospital, cooking, and generally everything. Then she thought of a question.

"What do your female warriors wear?"

"I guess they look more like human women, but they also have protective clothing on, so they look like warriors," Gormon replied.

Okay, so maybe she looked like a warrior without their protective gear on.

"Gormon, when you look at my spirit or aura or whatever you use to assess someone's species, do I appear human?"

"Yes."

"When I use an invisibility spell and exit this car, do I leave anything behind that says what I just did?" Stephanie asked, doing exactly what she said.

When she returned to the car, Gormon said "Yes and no. I

couldn't see you, but it was a sweep of something that went out with you. Once you closed the door, there was nothing left of you."

"Okay, I think we can sum this up as Ramsey was looking for fae folk in my house. I confused him by being human, and depending on where his eyes were focused, he may or may not have noticed me practicing magic. Since you can sense where he is on Earth, I guess it is not surprising that Ramsey can sense where you are. I wonder if he knew you were near his building earlier."

"Is it safe to go home?" Amelia asked.

"I've looked at the interior cameras in the house and I didn't see him anywhere. Can you sense if anyone magical is in my home, Gormon?"

"No one is there. He must have portaled back to where he is staying. I am not surprised. If I were him and trying to take over this world. I would first try to understand the world geographically, then I would explore other magical beings I could sense to see if they were possible allies or warriors from the Elven Republic after me. Did he appear shortly after we left?"

"I would guess about ten to fifteen minutes. Someday I'm going to teach Earth time and distance. About the same amount of time as we've sitting here in my car."

"Perhaps he was hoping to search your house once the warrior was gone from it," Gormon offered. "If I were him, I would worry that the Elven Republic will catch up to him."

Stephanie put her car in gear, and they returned home in no time. She had Gormon and Michael check out the house to make sure it was clear, then she and Amelia entered. The food she pulled out for dinner was sitting on the counter. She looked at her watch and decided it was still safe to eat and went to work cooking.

Gormon sat down on the couch and looked at the options he had. Finally, he stood up and said, "I think you and Amelia should return to the Elven Republic for your own safety. Ramsey has the power to kill you and he got close to you tonight."

# Chapter Nineteen

Stephanie thought about Gormon's statement while she chopped tomatoes and mushrooms. Then she shook her head "no."

"Look, I get that he's dangerous and killed your king. How did he do that?"

"He ground up iron into a small powder and served it to the king in his ale. Iron is bad for elves; it burns us and lessens our magic."

"Ouch. How did he get close enough to the king to do that? Didn't you know he was a dark warlock? Can you sense when a fae is bad? Is their energy or aura different?" Stephanie asked, making a mental note to move iron out of her house for Gormon and Michael or use it as a weapon the next time she met Ramsey. She had a cast iron skillet, and rather than using a cooking knife which had little iron in it, she instead should have taken a swing at Ramsey with the pan.

"We do not have many warlocks in our world. Warlocks are humans that in our history wandered into our world. They learn to direct the power in our world. We have both good and bad warlocks. They can disguise themselves and fool people. There is no difference in my senses as it is his soul that is bad. That is how he murdered the king. We were aware of a warlock amassing power and followers. However, he disguised himself as a servant and poisoned the king's ale. When we found out, the first warrior was killed by his power strikes—he can fling lightning bolts at you. That is what made him so difficult to capture. We had never seen that kind of power from a human before in the history of the realm. Unfortunately, it distorted his soul, making him believe he should rule over everything."

Stephanie made a note to herself that since Ramsey was human, to forget the cast iron skillet. And anyway, she wanted their eventual battle to take place outside of her house and preferably in a deserted wet area where he couldn't start too many things on fire with his lightning bolts.

"Did your prior king look down upon warlocks as they are only human?" Amelia asked, knowing about the prejudices of that king from Michael.

"You are starting to understand our prior king. Yes, he did. As I look back at that time in history, I wonder how many of our battles throughout the kingdom were caused by his attitude. Thankfully, he did not pass those prejudices on to his son, and our more recent two centuries have been much more peaceful."

"Does your realm have an antidote to iron poisoning? We have treatments here for the occasional iron poisoning, but they wouldn't work on the symptoms you've described," Stephanie asked.

"That is a good question and one I'll find the answer to from Nienna."

"So what's our game plan with Ramsey?" Michael asked. "Do we continue to ignore him and concentrate on retrieving the other prisoners first, or do we sit down with the warriors council and plan an attack?"

"What about the grimoire? It seems like something he would want to steal as it would bring power to him," Amelia asked.

Stephanie walked over to where she was keeping the book. She had buried it in a drawer under a blanket. She didn't often have guests inside her home, but on the off chance she did, she didn't want to have to remember that the book needed to be hidden. She initially was going to put the book where she found it underneath her medical school books, but she found it to be a pain moving the books from above it.

She sighed with relief. "It's still here. Should I move it somewhere safer, or what is safe from you magical people?"

"It is fine. Ramsey had the opportunity to steal it and did not. The book is strange—it wants to hide itself. Sometimes I can sense it and other times I cannot. It is a sentient being and wants to stay in safe and good hands," Gormon said.

"Wow," Amelia and Stephanie said at the same time and then smiled at each other.

"Okay, we're not going to hide in your realm. We've agreed to help you retrieve the remaining groups of prisoners outside of Ramsey, then we'll have a meeting in the Elven Republic to create a plan for capturing Ramsey. In the interim, is there anything you can do to put some kind of shield around this house, and perhaps I can ask the grimoire if it has a protection shield for Amelia and me."

Gormon stared at her for what seemed like a long time, then relaxed his stance minutely and nodded. Michael asked, "What's for dinner?"

She appreciated his breaking the tense moments. He was a very good man. "Chicken parmesan, garlic bread, brussel sprouts in seasoning with bacon, and ice cream for dessert."

"Maybe you can make a menu of things you cook, and I can order from you when I set up my delivery business."

"Not a chance, Michael. My schedule is too unpredictable. Give me another twenty minutes and I'll be ready to serve. Maybe you folks can find a protection spell in the grimoire while I finish our meal."

The three of them sat down with the grimoire. Gormon showed Amelia how to find wishful spells in it. They examined the spell the book provided and decided it was perfect for the house. Amelia then followed the directions. Michael stepped outside, but couldn't walk far or portal back inside due to the shield around the house, and thus they knew it worked.

Stephanie was ready to serve the meal by the time they had finished. As they sat down, she asked, "If it works to keep Michael out, it will work on Ramsey too, right?"

"I think so, but we have a good warlock in the Elven Republic, and I will see if he can break it later just to confirm."

"Okay. Tomorrow, do you want to go after the prisoners who have moved far away from here?" Stephanie asked.

"They will likely not be dangerous to humans. I think they are another couple of fae inappropriately sent to prison. Their crime was being mixed-species and not cleaning the palace to the prior king's specifications."

"Seriously, this king deserved to be overthrown. He was a rotten person to send people to jail for two centuries over inadequate cleaning. Did you warriors know what he was doing?" Amelia asked.

"No, or we might have intervened. The prison manager was the one who knew, and he was terrified that if he bucked the king he would end up in prison himself."

"That's really sad. Your prior king's actions created its own set of criminals and monsters. Is there anything in place to stop that from happening again?" Amelia asked.

"Yes, King Kanruil has created a justice system over the last century and a half after he found he did not enjoy sitting in judgment of his people. He wanted more voices determining justice for bad behavior. He did not enjoy the power of being the single voice of judgment. He would have fixed this prison on Earth, but he did not know about it and never thought to ask where Ramsey was as he had many tough months after his father was murdered."

"Still, we should approach this couple and take them back to the Elven Republic if they want. Perhaps they miss their family," Stephanie said.

"True. We will find them tomorrow first and see if they want to be portaled home," Gormon said. "Then we will return here and work on the remaining five criminals on the loose. Tomorrow will be a day of extremes with the nicest fae in the morning to the challenge of a shapeshifting wyvern in the afternoon."

"Oh my gosh. This is going to be epic!" Amelia said.

"Forget epic, we could die by being clawed to death. Isn't that how wyverns kill?" Stephanie asked.

"Or they pick you up and drop you from great heights," Michael said.

"We could use the same protective umbrella we did with the Korrigans," Stephanie suggested.

"They have powerful magic, and I would guess the claws would go through our umbrella, or failing that it could squash us," Gormon said.

"Aren't you all rays of sunshine?" Amelia said. "How do you propose capturing this one? You say they are shapeshifters on top of having twenty ways to kill you. Why was it sent to prison?"

"Somehow, Ramsey harnessed its flying power and was able to attack various cities in the kingdom with its help. We sliced it up with many warrior swords, then our healers stepped in and sedated the creature, healed it, and sent it to prison."

"It's interesting the wyvern decided not to follow Ramsey from prison. What's it been doing the last few days, quietly sitting in the forest?"

"Yes."

"You said the wyvern was a shapeshifter. What does it shift into?" Amelia asked.

"A humanoid-looking creature."

"So could it shift into a human and then you might walk right by it, or can you smell it and know it's wyvern? Can you reason with the creature when it's in either shape?" Stephanie asked.

"I would be able to tell that it is a shapeshifter, but not necessarily a wyvern. There are so few in our realm that it is not a scent I am familiar with."

"So, we need to chat with it while it's in human form, or can you telepathically talk to it?" Stephanie asked.

"No, I cannot talk to a wyvern when it is in its beast form."

"How did Ramsey speak with it enough to gain control?"

"I think he cast a spell upon it with his wand."

"Let me look through the grimoire and see if there's a spell that might work with this species," Amelia said, flipping through the book.

"Sweetie, close your eyes and think about what we need. We want a protection spell, and we want it to shift to its humanoid form so we can converse," Stephanie said.

Amelia did as her mother directed. She laid the book open in her lap with her hand underneath the back cover.

The three of them watched as the pages began to move, then stay open on one page.

"Open your eyes now, Amelia. The grimoire may have a spell for us."

She opened her eyes and read the spell. "I'm too much of a novice witch to have a clue if this works. So either Mom and I will be eaten alive by the wyvern tomorrow or we'll have a robust conversation."

"Amelia, you and I are not going together to spell this wyvern. At least one of us needs to remain alive. You will wait at the car even if I have to spell you to do that or have Gormon take you to the Elven Republic for your own safety. If the wyvern is reasonable, we'll bring you in; if not, we'll be in a fight for our lives and I'll do a better job if I'm not worrying about your safety," Stephanie said, in her stern mom voice that brokered no compromise.

Amelia was worried about her mom, but she knew she could get Gormon to move her to the Elven Republic if need be, so she acknowledged that she would play by the rules.

Stephanie cleaned up the dishes despite Gormon's offering to clean them the elven way. The warrior was using his senses to check on Ramsey's location. He would also admit to himself that the wyvern could be the death of all of them tomorrow. He would notify the realm so it would be ready to send more warriors if the three of them perished. Michael and he meditated while the humans slept that night, or at least tried to sleep. Tomorrow was a heavy day when their lives were going to be at the biggest risk since this mission started.

The next morning Stephanie prepared a hearty breakfast for the four of them. Then Gormon checked on the location of the mixed-species couple before opening a portal to take them close by. The couple had managed to head south to the Baja Peninsula of Mexico. It was warm and humid, and the two men immediately looked out of place in their flowing robes.

"Can you try and fit in here by changing your clothing and hiding the swords?" Stephanie asked.

"We'll just cloak ourselves. We're looking for a small couple —perhaps a foot tall each. Green skin, wrinkled faces," Gormon said.

"They would stand out here on the beach. Are they perhaps over in those rocks?" Amelia asked, pointing to a rocky outcropping.

When Gormon and Michael used their invisibility spells, Amelia and her mother had automatically used their own spells so they could see the men. They had stopped in the sand and Gormon appeared to be conversing telepathically with someone, given the look of concentration on his face. Finally, he moved closer.

They were looking for a part-dwarf, part-imp species. As they got closer to the rocks, Stephanie finally saw them. The entire time, Gormon must have been talking to the pair.

He said out loud, "This is Michael, also a mixed species who was in the prison. King Kanruil pardoned him. You can chat with him for verification. This is Dr. Stephanie Jones, a human healer from Earth, and her daughter Amelia. They are both newly discovered witches helping us navigate Earth and round up prisoners. Sadly, some of your fellow prisoners have harmed humans and Dr. Jones has had to treat them."

Michael then spoke to the couple. "What Lord Warrior Gormon Mialynn says is true. I was imprisoned because I had thoughts of killing that old bully king. He made life so difficult for us mixed species. His son is a much better king and you'll be welcome home and issued a pardon for ending up in jail."

The woman of the couple spoke and said, "We have family we would like to connect with. How long were we in that prison? We came here as it was too cold where that prison was located."

Michael replied, "I'm sorry to inform you, but we were in that prison for two centuries. My human mother died while I was there, but my father is still alive."

Stephanie saw the woman shed tears and throw her arms around the man. Gormon whispered to her, "Their species lives probably 250 years, so they lost family that they will never see. They want to portal home, so let me escort them. Michael will see you home and I will join you there."

They nodded and walked through different portals to get to different locations. Anyone on the beach watching probably assumed they had drunk too much alcohol, or the sun was creating an illusion of people appearing and disappearing.

# Chapter Twenty

When they arrived at Stephanie's house, she made lunch for them and then practiced the wyvern spell in the grimoire a couple of times. She reinforced with her daughter that she would be staying by the car or Gormon would run her to the Elven Republic where she couldn't escape and try to be her mother's back-up. She had a sandwich waiting for Gormon when he arrived.

Stephanie was clear about keeping her daughter safe. "Gormon, can you sense if Amelia leaves the car and tries to move closer to us when we're dealing with the wyvern?"

"I can, and I will portal her to our realm if she moves."

"Good, let's go." This time they would drive. That way if anyone was injured, they could drive to help and they had a warm place for Amelia to await the outcome of their attempted conversation with the wyvern. An hour later, Stephanie was looking for a parking space near the forest where the wyvern was located. The grimoire had said how close she had to be to cast the spell to put the creature into its human form. Gormon suggested she start from one hundred yards away as the wyvern had good smelling skills and might realize there were humans nearby to eat.

Stephanie did exactly that. Nothing happened in the distance, so she called out, "Hey Mr. or Ms. Wyvern, can we talk?" They heard a confusion-tinged response, "Yeeessss?"

They approached closer to find a naked woman shivering in the cold. So, the wyvern was a female. She had black hair and a bluish tinge to her skin, likely from the cold. She was slightly taller than the average woman at close to six feet.

Gormon cast a spell and soon had a cloak in his hand to put over the woman.

"I'm sorry, I cast a spell to have you shapeshift into a humanoid shape forgetting about the cold. My name is Stephanie and I'm a human healer from Earth, and I'm also a witch. Can we talk to you in this form?"

"What do you want? I'm not joining your party to take over this world or another. I just want to be left in peace."

"Would you like to return to the Elven Republic?" Gormon asked. He knew that this species was one of the shortest-lived species from his world, averaging just one hundred years.

"How long was I in that prison?"

"Two centuries."

The wyvern put her chin down on her chest. Then she said, "Then my two eggs that the warlock stole from me are long dead and gone."

"What's your name?" Stephanie asked.

"Onyx. I was named for the black hair on my head."

"Onyx. There were many injustices to the fae serving out prison sentences. It seems like you assisted Ramsey as he held your future children hostage."

"Yes. I would never have tried to kill the king. I didn't like him, but I was living a peaceful life sitting on my nest in a cave outside the city of Cavebeach. When I was out hunting for food, I came back to find my eggs gone and Ramsey waiting. He'd moved my eggs into hiding and said I had to take him on as a rider or he would smash my eggs. I should have known this would never work out."

"How often do wyvern produce eggs?" Stephanie asked, not having a clue as to the reproductive abilities of wyvern or, indeed, any fae.

"Several times in our lifetime, but the problem is finding a mate. I'm a lightning wyvern and can only mate with another lightning wyvern."

"Do you wish to return home so you can begin over, possibly find a new mate, or just live near another wyvern? I believe you are the only one on Earth, so if you stay here, there will be no more children for you," Stephanie said.

"I want to stay here long enough to kill Ramsey as he killed my eggs. Then I'll return to the Elven Republic to find a new mate," Onyx said.

"Do you have a plan on how to kill Ramsey?" Michael asked.

While Michael asked questions, Stephanie let Amelia know it was safe to join them.

"I was going to pick him up in my claws and drop him from a high place."

"How long can you stay shifted as a human?" Stephanie asked.

"I can stay shifted as long as I need."

"Would you like to come home with us to a warm place and food? Your wyvern form wouldn't fit inside my house, but your human form does."

She paused a while to think about this strange group of fae and humans. She decided that while she was a cave-dwelling member of the dragon family, in her human form she would appreciate a warm place and some food. Maybe she would learn where Ramsey was and how she could get to him first. They didn't seem keen on killing him; rather, these people wanted to send him back to prison. That wasn't good enough for her. She would regain her strength from the long hibernation, learn what had happened during the last two hundred years, and then make her plans to kill the evil warlock. She nodded and they walked through the forest.

Her feet were bare, but they were warming up. She wondered if the warrior had cast a spell. She didn't feel the cold when she was in her other form, but as a human without covering, she'd been cold. They reached the car and the other fae warned her not to pay attention to the road. It was so strange to speed down the path in a metal box. She much preferred flying. On their way home, they stopped for food at a barbecue restaurant.

"Do you eat for your human size or your wyvern size?"

"My wyvern size. I eat lots of animals and fish."

Stephanie nodded and ordered food for ten people, figuring Onyx would eat enough for several humans.

They arrived home and the fae seemed to go crazy at the same time. All three ran out of the car and into the house. Stephanie was left staring at her daughter, wondering what they had run out for. She started gathering up the food to bring it inside.

The three fae were standing at her kitchen counter discussing what they had sensed. Michael and Onyx were quickly diverted by the food smells when all the bags had been brought in from the car.

Onyx hadn't spent enough time in human form to learn manners, and so she tore through several bags eating amazing amounts of food. She had guessed as a shapeshifter she could eat for her larger form. It reminded Stephanie of Nathan's famous hotdog-eating contest held on the fourth of July. To watch the contestants scarf down so many hot dogs was nause-ating to watch. Oh well. She'd rather the wyvern eat BBQ ribs than pieces of her flesh.

While Stephanie was tired from the drive and the spell to change Onyx to her human form, the hunger of the wyvern really put her off her own food, and so she asked, "Why did you three jump out of my car?" She thought she knew the answer, but she waited for what they had to say.

"We sensed and smelled Ramsey in your house," Gormon replied.

"So your shield didn't work."

"No. Ramsey is a powerful warlock, and he took down the shield."

"I thought you were monitoring his location?" Stephanie said.

"I have to reach out and sense his location. I'll admit, I assumed my shield would work and I was not as diligent tracking him. I was also distracted by Onyx's feelings about the food. I thought she was going to dive over the seat at any moment and attack you for the food."

Stephanie hadn't realized she was in any danger. No wonder Gormon was distracted. Then she had a thought and ran to the drawer where the grimoire was kept. She pulled the blanket off and it was gone.

"The grimoire is gone," she said upon her return. "Can you sense it anywhere in the house?"

Gormon stood quiet and let his senses search. He didn't sense it in the house. He shook his head.

"I thought you said it was a sentient being that would rather stay with a good person. Why would it go with Ramsey? Was it his book two hundred years ago? We never did figure out why it ended up at my house."

Gormon looked deeply disturbed over the loss of the book.

Stephanie suspected there was something he hadn't told her about the book, but if it was so special, why hadn't he done a better job protecting it?

"I need to meet in the Elven Republic and discuss the loss of the grimoire with the king and council. You cannot join me in these meetings, but I would prefer for your safety that all of you join me in my world as my shield hasn't worked."

Amelia and Stephanie looked at each other, then Stephanie nodded her head in agreement, as did Onyx.

"We'll go," Stephanie announced.

The End

*Follow the adventures of Stephanie and Gormon in the next book of the Stephanie Jones series due out later in 2024.*

# Map of the Elven Republic

# About the Author

A. Peche has been primarily a mystery and thriller author up to this series under the name Alec Peche. I enjoy reading the Mystery and Urban Fantasy genres. My trusty dog and cat are nearby whether reading or writing. I enjoy the diversity of the world and I'm always watching people and events for story ideas. All of my stories are generated by my imagination, I don't use AI to write books.

If you would like to sign up for my bi-weekly blog and announcement of new books, please follow this link: https://www.AlecPecheBooks.com

While you're waiting for the next story, if you would be so kind as to leave a review for this book, that would be great. I appreciate all the feedback and support. Reviews buoy my spirits and stoke the fires of creativity.

# Also by A. Peche

**Jill Quint, MD Forensic Pathologist Series**

Time's Up (prequel short story)

Vials

Chocolate Diamonds

A Breck Death

Death On A Green

A Taxing Death

Murder At The Podium

Castle Killing

Crescent City Murder

Sicilian Murder

Opus Murder

Forensic Murder

Return to the Scene of the Crime (short story)

Embers of Murder

Ashes to Murder

Mint Death

**Damian Green Series**

Red Rock Island

Willow Glen Heist

The Girl From Diana Park

Evergreen Valley Murder

Long Delayed Justice

**<u>Michelle Watson Series</u>**

Now You Don't See Me

Where Did She Go?

How Did She Get There?

**<u>Dog Humor</u>**

Eat, Play, Poop: Letters to my parents from camp

**<u>A. Peche</u>**

**<u>New Urban Fantasy Series - Stephanie Jones</u>**

The Awakening at Lake Tahoe (short story)

Witch's Medicine